* * * * *

To Maureen

my wife, closest companion and dearest friend

* * * * *

ALSO BY MICHAEL C. COX

* * * * *

NOVELS

Once Upon A Term

* * * * *

SHORT STORIES

Facts and Fantasies – Volume 2

Facts and Fantasies – Volume 3

Facts and Fantasies – Volume 4

Facts and Fantasies – Omnibus

* * * * *

Facts and Fantasies

Volume 1

Cedar of Lebanon

Michael C. Cox

Mimast Inc

Mimast Inc

* * * * *

This book is a work of fiction. Names, characters, businesses, organizations, places, events, and incidents either are the product of the author's imagination or are used fictitiously. Any resemblance to actual persons, living or dead, events or locales is entirely coincidental.

* * * * *

Acknowledgements

Firstly, I must acknowledge a debt to the teachers who taught English language and English literature in my first five years at a Grammar school in my home town of Bristol. In spite of their efforts and best intentions, by the time I was sixteen I had acquired a taste for reading but not for writing. To be fair to those teachers, I felt at the time that I had so much to read and so little to write about.

I must acknowledge two of those teachers: Alex Mair, a Scotsman no less, and A.B. Reynolds, a somewhat eccentric Englishman. The former opened my eyes to literature by telling me to read Great Expectations by Charles Dickens. The latter opened my eyes to language by telling me to read out loud the first sentence in an exercise on syntax error: "Do not kill your wife with work, let electricity do it."

Secondly, I must thank my dear friend, Leif G. Stolee. He has encouraged me to write about people and events that have enriched my life over the past few decades. Leif's enthusiastic response to my stories has kept me at my computer and out of mischief. And I must mention here, James Stolee. He tempered his brother's enthusiasm with many well deserved criticisms of my writings.

Lastly but certainly not least, I must thank my wife, Maureen. She has always been my dearest and closest friend. She has watched over my grammar, corrected my spelling and made many constructive suggestions. Without Maureen's love and support, I doubt that I could ever have written a single word.

* * * * *

Needless to say, any mistakes in grammar and spelling, and any errors in facts used fictitiously, are my fault entirely. Nobody else is to blame.

* * * * *

THE FOUR STORIES

* * * * *

* * * * *

Author's note

These four short stories combine factual episodes and figments of my imagination in varied proportions. I have tried accurately to reveal the facts underlying all four stories but my memory is not what it was. In three of the stories, I have also tried to conceal the identities of the people involved. If I failed in the latter and thereby upset any family members, friends, colleagues or acquaintances, may I point out I never intended to embarrass and, more often than not, the law seems to benefit lawyers rather than litigants.

THE LAWN

This story is a fiction based upon facts personally reported to me and upon events I experienced firsthand. For instance, I knew a chemist, who left a major chemical company, solved a pollution problem, published a book of walks to unusual places, brewed his own wine and who, inspired by the fall of a cast iron gutter that might have killed his son, made his fortune in PVC guttering and downpipes.

* * * * *

One secret of success in life is for a man to be ready for his opportunity when it comes - Benjamin Disraeli.

* * * * *

'I quit!'

'What?'

'You heard me.'

'But Harry…'

Dr Harold Procter stormed out of the laboratory and strode down the corridor leaving the heavy fire door to spring shut on his open-mouthed colleague.

'Hello! This is Dr Robinson. Put me through to Mr Harper.'

'I'm sorry Dr Robinson but Mr Harper is tied up and…'

'Well you'd better untie him, Pamela. This is urgent. It's about Dr Procter.'

'What about Dr Procter?'

'Just put me through. Now, please Pam!'

All that Frank Robinson could tell Donald Harper, the general manager of HG Chemicals Ltd, was that the Company's senior analytical chemist had blown his top and stormed off, saying he was leaving.

'What did he say exactly?'

'I quit,' said Frank.

'Is that all?'

'Well,' said Frank reluctantly, 'that was the last thing he said.'

'OK. What did he say before that?'

'He said… He said… Harper can stuff it! I've no idea what it was. Sorry. In the five years I've worked with Harry I've never known him to blow his top. Have you any idea what got into him?'

'It may be something that's been brewing for a while now,' Harper said hesitantly.

'Nothing I've said or done… or not done, I hope.'

'Absolutely not, Frank. Nothing to do with you at all. I'm quite sure of that.'

'He'll probably walk in on Monday morning as though nothing has happened.'

'What? Oh, yes, yes,' said Harper, putting out of his mind the clash he had with Harry earlier that afternoon. 'Look, Frank, just in case Harry doesn't come back, I'm putting you in charge of the laboratories for now, OK?'

Dr Harold Procter never did return to HG chemicals. Dr Frank Robinson became the senior analytical chemist in charge of the laboratories his predecessor had planned in meticulous detail, had equipped with the latest instrumentation and had run efficiently to the most exacting standards for the past five years. Neither Frank, who enjoyed the increased responsibility and salary, nor Donald, whose straws had finally broken Harry's back, gave any thought to how their former colleague would earn a living. That was his business. It was no concern of theirs.

* * * * *

'You're home early. Anything wrong?'

'No. Why do you say that?'

'You're never home before 5 o'clock and...'

'And…?'

'You've come home empty-handed.'

9

'What do you mean *empty-handed*?'

'I asked you to get a couple of bottles of wine to go with the meal this evening.'

'We've got plenty of wine…'

'I've told you before, Harry, I'm not serving our guests with your *home-made plonk.*'

Dr Harold Procter was very proud of his wines which never deserved to be denigrated as home-made plonk. When he didn't respond to her denigration with his usual *I'll have you know that I'm as professional about wine-making as I am about chemistry, etc., etc., etc.,* his wife was rather surprised. When Harry went quietly away and returned about forty minutes later with two bottles of Cabernet Sauvignon, two bottles of Muscadet de Sevre-et-Maine, a bottle of Harvey's Bristol Cream sherry and a bottle of Mercier Brut Champagne to drink with the pear crumble and the biscuits and cheese, Joy could not believe her eyes.

'What on earth…'

'Put these three in the fridge,' Harry said, handing Joy the Muscadet and Champagne, 'while I pour us a glass of sherry.'

'Are you feeling alright?'

'Santé!' said Harry, clinking glasses. 'Anything I can do to help?'

'Now I *know* you're not well,' said Joy. 'Go and watch the news on the telly.'

'No thanks. I've had enough gloom and doom for one day. I'll do the lawn.'

'If you really want to be helpful, perhaps you would empty the dishwasher and lay the table before you go into the garden.'

'No sooner said than done,' said Harry, draining his glass.

After he had emptied the dishwasher and set the table, Harry went outside and mowed his beloved lawn. Dr Harold Procter had three hobbies – his wife called them obsessions - which he pursued with the seriousness of a true professional. The first was Analytical Chemistry. 'Oh, no, Frank, you're quite wrong,' he once said to Dr Robinson. 'What I do here at HG Chemicals Ltd is *not* my *job*; it's my *hobby*. I'm just lucky I get paid for it.'

The second hobby was wine – making it, analysing it, bottling it and, of course, drinking it. He usually gave colleagues, including even the general manager, a bottle or two of his wine for Christmas. 'I'm glad you found the wine acceptable, Donald, but you're quite wrong,' he once said to the general manager, 'the red was not a Bordeaux; it was a blend of two separate wines: rhubarb and elderberry; the white was made from blackcurrants and over-ripe bananas.'

The third hobby was his lawn; it was his pride and joy.

Almost two hours elapsed from the time that Harry emptied the dishwasher to the time that Trevor and Dorothy Partridge rang the front door bell and he let them in. When Trevor asked Harry if they could stroll down the garden to the river's edge, Dot made a beeline for the kitchen to chat with Joy. 'Is your Harry alright? I only ask because he seemed… well… different somehow.'

11

Joy had sensed that something was wrong with Harry but she couldn't quite put her finger on it. He kept getting under her feet wanting to help in her kitchen; she was glad when he went out to do his lawn. When Joy asked her long-standing friend exactly how Harry had *seemed different*, Dot said, 'I don't know really. He seemed to have something on his mind. Oh, it's probably just my imagination. Trevor often seems a bit odd when he comes home late from work on Friday. Take today for instance. He was really miserable, moaning on about red-tape and a busybody inspector just out of college. But as soon as I reminded him we were coming here, he was back to his old cheerful self straight away. Funny that!'

'If your lawn didn't slope down to the river, you could play bowls on it, old man,' said Trevor. 'How do you keep it like this? Chemical fertilizers and herbicides I suppose.'

'I've told you before,' said Harry. 'It's more to do with how I prepared the ground, the seed I used and when I sowed it. As for what you usually call *those killer chemicals*, I've only once used copper sulphate; that was on a persistent bit of moss.'

'I read somewhere that per square foot of garden, a lawn takes the most time and effort; a bed of roses takes the least,' said Trevor.

'No doubt that's why you dug up your lawn to grow roses, you lazy blighter!'

'You said it. No aerating, scarifying, feeding, weeding, watering and mowing for me, thank you very much,' retorted Trevor. 'Just a bit of mulching, feeding, deadheading and light pruning now and then; that suits me down to the ground.'

'What about those aphids on the buds and that black spot on the leaves.'

'Easy,' said Trevor. 'I spray once or twice a year with systemic insecticide and copper sulphate fungicide... which reminds me... We've run into a problem at work.'

Trevor Partridge owned and ran Canford Mill Electroplating Ltd (CME), the company he inherited from his father and which he

12

joined straight from school at the age of eighteen. He complemented the practical experience he gained at CME with the distance learning courses of the Institute of Metal Finishing. Trevor married Dorothy when he was twenty three. Four years and two daughters later he qualified as a Licentiate of the Institute.

'Let me guess. The Rivers (Prevention of Pollution) Act 1951?'

'That's what the young inspector kept quoting today,' said Trevor.

'I thought you stopped using cyanide complexes in your plating baths.'

'Yes, we did. Ages ago. It's nothing to do with cyanide. It's heavy metals in our waste water. According to the latest regulation, dissolved copper ought to be below 0.005 mg per litre. I've been given two weeks to deal with this. Any ideas?'

'Maybe,' said Harry. 'I've been looking at ion exchange recently and...'

'Look here Harry, I need your help,' interrupted Trevor, not really listening to his friend. 'Any chance you can get away from HG Chemicals for a couple of days?'

'I don't see why not.'

'Really? Well that would be...'

'What are friends for?' interrupted Harry. 'Let's go indoors. I think the food's ready.'

Joy was a first class cook. When Harry teased her by saying cooking was just a pastime and hobby, she rose to the bait. 'Hobby indeed! I'll have you know it's a full-time *unpaid* job satisfying your appetite, Dr Procter.' That evening the four friends enjoyed a starter of garlic mushrooms in batter followed by salmon steak amandine, asparagus tips and herb sautéed potatoes. Pear crumble followed by a choice of cheeses was accompanied by a glass of chilled champagne, made from a blend of 15% Chardonnay, 45% Pinot Noir and 40% Pinot Meunier grapes. When Dot raised her glass of the golden nectar and asked what they were celebrating, Joy said, 'I've no idea. You'd better ask Harry.'

* * * * *

On Monday morning, Harry and Jonathon, his teen-age son, left the house together as usual. Harry opened the garage door and drove off. Jonathon closed the garage door and hopped on his bicycle. When he saw his father's car turn left instead of right at the end of the road he didn't think it odd. His mind was elsewhere. When Joy was running the vacuum cleaner around Harry's study and saw he had left his briefcase on the chair behind his desk she didn't think it odd. Her mind was elsewhere.

'Trevor to reception, please,' announced the young lady over the Tannoy while Harry signed the book and clipped the visitors label to the lapel of his jacket.

'You made it then,' said Trevor hurrying down the stairs from his office; his *eagle's nest* as he called it because from there he could see almost everything that was going on in the works. 'Let's not waste any of your valuable time. Follow me and I'll show you our latest set up.' Then turning to the receptionist he said, 'Tell Joan I'm in the plant with Doctor Procter and ask her to arrange for coffee in my office at 10 o'clock.'

'Joan still looking after you and keeping your desk tidy then,' said Harry.

'Same way she looked after my dad. We couldn't do without her.'

Trevor and Harry spent the next ninety minutes in the main plating room discussing both the theory and the practice of commercial electroplating – a world away from Jonathon Procter's simple electrolysis experiments at school where he just collected two pieces of copper foil from his science teacher, connected them to a 6-volt battery and stuck them into the copper sulphate solution in his glass beaker.

14

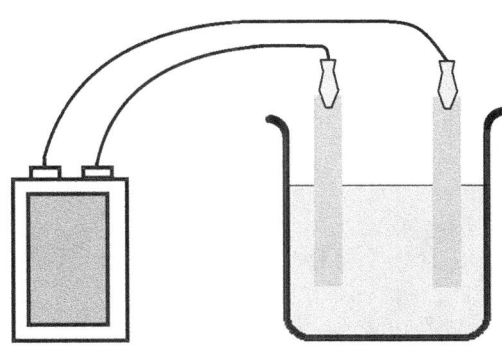

At CME all surfaces for plating had to be thoroughly degreased and cleaned. This often involved several stages and a variety of chemicals that included caustic potash (for degreasing) and special mixtures of acids (hydrochloric, nitric and sulphuric) in various proportions. After the electroplating – a process that itself could involve several stages – the surfaces would still be subjected to treatment with acid mixtures before any final washing with water. Harry was particularly interested in where the acid mixtures came from and where the final washes went.

At 10 o'clock precisely, Joan served coffee in Trevor's eagle's nest then left the two men seated in comfortable chairs facing one another. Harry came quickly to the point. 'I could solve your effluent problem and get the inspector off your back in under two weeks. It shouldn't cost much to set up and maintain. I'll give you a list of materials I'll need and start work right away.' When Trevor asked what HG Chemicals would have to say, Harry gave his friend a strange look and said, 'I don't think they'll miss me.'

For the next two weeks Harry left home in the morning and returned in the late afternoon at his usual time. He spent most of the day at CME installing and testing his ion exchange units. He and Trevor usually had morning coffee in the eagle's nest to discuss progress but they switched to afternoon tea on two occasions when Harry had meetings with his lawyer, Frederick York, of Trevanion, Oxley and York. On two other afternoons, Harry left CME early to inspect some old abandoned buildings that had served as a German prison-of-war camp during World War II.

'Harry, you saved my bacon. These ion exchangers you've installed remove every trace of dissolved copper. It's absolutely brilliant,' enthused Trevor. 'You should have seen the look on that young inspector's face this morning.' It was Harry's second and last Friday afternoon at CME. The two men were drinking tea in Trevor's office.

'Think nothing of it. It's the least I could do for a friend.'

'You are a friend indeed, Harry but this is also business. There's the matter of your fee as well as compensation for the time you've missed at HG Chemicals. What do I owe you.'

'Nothing at all, Trevor. Like I said, HG Chemicals won't have missed me.'

'They won't miss their senior analyst! Rubbish! Anyway, friend or no friend, you're entitled to a consultancy fee. Name your figure.'

Trevor, I don't want a fee but if you insist on showing your appreciation, I have a suggestion.'

'Fire away.'

'Give me the exclusive contract to supply you with the acid mixtures for your plating and washing baths. I'll save you anything up to ten percent on your present costs.'

'How could you save me ten percent, Harry?' said Trevor with a frown. 'We get everything direct from ICI.'

'I know. Don't worry, Trevor, I can undercut Imperial Chemical Industries.'

'OK, Harry. I trust you. You're on. How soon can you make your first delivery?'

* * * * *

'You're home early. That's the third Friday in a row. What's going on?' asked Joy.

16

'I've got something to tell you. Come into the lounge. I'll pour you a glass of sherry. You might need it.' When they were sitting comfortably, Harry dropped his bombshell.

'You're joking. You *must be joking*.'

'It's no joke, Joy. I left HG Chemicals two weeks ago.'

'So where have you been going for the past two weeks?'

'I've been helping Trevor at Canford Mill Electroplating to…'

'So that's it. You're working for Trevor now. I hope he's paying you more than HG Chemicals. We could do with a bit extra now that…'

'No! No, Joy, I'm not working for CME. I'm on the dole. I'm unemployed.'

'You'd better pour me another sherry. The next thing you'll be telling me is that I'll have to go back to work.'

'Well I suppose that's true in a way,' said Harry. 'I'd better explain.'

Joy listened as Harry told her his plan. They would form a private company to provide Trevor with the specialized acid mixtures and chemicals CME needed. And no, they would not be messing about in her kitchen. The company would occupy the old prisoner-of-war camp. The company would buy the separate acids and chemicals at a fair trade price from Imperial Chemical Industries. Harry himself – perhaps with help from Jonathon at weekends – would mix the acids and chemicals. The company would sell the mixtures to CME at a fair mark up but for less than Trevor was paying ICI. Harry would be a director and general manager. Joy would be the company secretary and treasurer. Simple!

'Gamble, I think you mean,' said Joy. 'Procter and gamble… now where have I…'

'Droll! Very droll! You'll be turning this into a soap opera next,' said Harry.

'I don't follow you,' said Joy, genuinely puzzled.

'P&G, one of the world's largest multinational corporations, was founded in 1837 in Ohio by two immigrants; Bill Procter, a candle maker from England, and Jim Gamble, a soap maker from Ireland. In the roaring twenties, Procter & Gamble, famous for its Ivory floating soap, sponsored a series of radio programs that became known as soap operas.'

'I'm just trying to be realistic, Harry. *You* might not think it's a gamble but... well I don't think it's simple. For a start, how long does it take to form a company?'

'One day according to Freddy York,' said Harry.

'Oh, really,' said Joy. 'you've seen our lawyer. Alright. How much will it cost?'

'According to Freddy York, under £100.'

'Oh!' said Joy, taking a sip of her sherry. 'What about planning permission for the buildings; how long will that take to get?'

'Now that,' said Harry. 'is another story altogether. I rang the bell three times before anybody in the planning department came to help me. While I was waiting I couldn't help noticing the sign on the wall behind the counter.'

THERE'S NO REASON FOR IT. IT'S JUST OUR POLICY.

'As long as it doesn't take too long,' said Harry, 'it won't be a problem because Trevor will go on getting his mixtures from ICI until we are up and running.'

'What will all this cost and what are we going to live on in the meantime?'

'Well, I was hoping you could tap Walter for a loan.'

'I wouldn't even dream of asking my father,' snapped Joy.

'I was afraid of that. So as company director, secretary and treasurer, you'd better work your charms on our bank manager.'

'I think I need another sherry,' said Joy.

Joy Procter was always the epitome of elegance even when, in her words, she was slaving over a hot cooker. When she stepped into Barclands bank, she caused heads to turn. Joy was tall, upright and slim but not thin. Her naturally black hair was neatly brushed and firmly held in a bun at the back of her head. Her makeup was skilfully applied to subtly enhance her fine features. The small jade brooch pinned at the throat of her white Victorian blouse matched the colour of her eyes; the grey of her trouser suit matched the touch of grey in her hair which, she well knew, wasn't caused by stress or worry. It was in her genes to go grey; her parents had grey hair in their early forties. Harry once explained that their melanocyte cells stopped making pigment so grey hair grew in place of the dark hairs when they fell out.

The somewhat portly manager of the local branch of the so-called *friendly listening* bank, gave Joy a reassuringly firm handshake and waited until she was comfortably seated in front of his desk before he took his own seat behind it. Joy was prepared for hostility and deafness. Instead, Thornton Metcalfe was avuncular and attentive as she presented her case for a loan and answered his questions about her company's structure, its articles of association and her business plan, copies of which she produced from her black leather portfolio case. He was particularly interested in her intention to renovate the old buildings on the site of the former prisoner-of-war camp.

'I'm sure that we can help finance your business venture, Mrs Procter, but…,' Thornton said with just the hint of a sigh, 'I fear the amount of credit Barclands can extend to your company...' He paused, placing his thumbs and finger tips together to form an arch, then continued, 'is strictly limited. You already have a first mortgage on your house.'

'I quite understand. It's just that…'

'Allow me to make a suggestion, Mrs Procter. Before you consider a second mortgage on your home, you might care to talk to the economic development officer at County Hall. I could give you her name. You might well qualify for a Commercial Premises Improvement and Security Grant and our local authority might well pay up to 75% of your cost of renovating that old POW camp.'

'Do you think so?' said Joy, striving to appear cool, calm and collected.

'Why not? You would be establishing a local industry and providing local employment even if it's just for you and your husband initially.'

'Thank you Mr Metcalfe. I'm very grateful for your help.'

'One other thing, dear lady,' said the manager, getting to his feet, 'you might consider selling a piece of your land for housing development.'

'Part of the old POW camp site, you mean?'

'Oh no, not that. I was thinking of where you live. You own the land freehold, I believe.'

It did take only one day to form and register H & J Chemical Distributors Ltd but it took much longer to raise the money, to obtain the planning permission and permits and to get just one of the buildings operational. Trevor and Jonathon helped at the weekends but it was Harry who did most of the renovating. According to Joy, he renovated himself with the physical effort; he lost any trace of midriff bulge and his weight fell to 170 pounds, ideal for his large frame and his height of just over 6 feet.

Joy kept a sharp eye on the cash flow but in spite of her skilful management, it became clear that the bank loan and the local authority grant would not see them through. They still had to renovate a second building and make it secure for storing the chemicals from ICI. They still had to buy a vehicle and equip it for delivering the rather dangerous acid mixtures to Canford Mill Electroplating. And they would, of course, have to pay the interest on the bank loan and the premiums on the various insurance policies; personal accident, public liability, etc. Much as she dreaded the thought, Joy would have to talk to Harry about his lawn.

'I've got something to tell you. Come into the lounge. I'll pour you a glass of sherry. You might need it.' When they were sitting comfortably, Joy dropped *her* bombshell.

'You're joking. You *must be joking*,' said Harry.

'It's no joke. This is the only way to raise the extra money we need.'

'But…'

'No buts, Harry. You'll have to sacrifice your lawn if our company is to survive.'

'I suppose you're going to sell my lawn, is that it?'

'Now that's a good point, Harry. I hadn't thought of that. Every penny helps.'

'So what's this cunning scheme of yours to do away with my lawn?' asked Harry.

'We'll gift your lawn and the land it covers to H & J Chemical Distributors Ltd. The company will sell the lawn as high quality turf - thank you for that idea, Harry – and sell the land to a builder on a 99 year lease which will bring the company in ground rent.'

'Who exactly is going to buy my lawn and our land?'

'I don't know yet,' said Joy. 'I haven't got that far.'

'Whose idea was this anyway?' said Harry. 'Trevor's?'

'No. If you must know it was something Thornton said to me.'

'Our bank manager?'

'Yes. Thornton Metcalfe.'

'So it's Thornton now, is it? Not Mr Metcalfe. Just how charming were you to him?'

'Now you're being silly. It was just his passing thought as I left his office. Anyway, I think we should sell the land for housing development – that was the term Thorn… Mr Metcalfe used.'

'I hate to admit it but you're right. I'll have to sacrifice the lawn but…'

'I said no buts, Harry.'

'*but first*,' said Harry, 'I think we should form another company.'

'Why on earth should we…'

'How about calling it H & J Builders Ltd? How does that sound to you?'

'I'm not with you, Harry. What's the idea?'

'We'll deed the land to H & J Chemical Distributors Ltd (HJCD). H & J Builders Ltd (HJB) will buy the land from HJCD on a 99 year lease and build a house on the land and sell the house leasehold at a profit.'

'So now you're going to build a house, is that it?'

'Yes my dear, that's the idea. Simple really!'

The new company was quickly formed and registered and the land quickly deeded to it. The lawn turf was quickly sold for much more than either Harry or Joy ever imagined. The plans of their existing house were quickly adapted and approved for the new house; building it was not so quick and not so simple. They do say *you get what you pay for*. Harry and Joy, as fledgling building contractors, certainly paid for what they got at the hands of the tradesmen and the building supplies merchants.

'I suppose you'll be wanting wire cut facing bricks for external work and engineering bricks for below ground and damp course,' said the poker-faced brickyard foreman.

'Yes, I think so,' said Joy already bewildered by the several hundred different types of brick available.

'What are you using for your internal walls, breeze block or commons?'

'I'm not sure,' said Joy. 'Which would you recommend?'

'Commons.'

'Why not breeze blocks?' asked Joy tentatively.

'We don't make 'em,' the foreman replied sourly.

'Oh!' was all that Joy could say.

'What colour facers do you want?'

'Which colour is the most popular?'

'We make and sell about ten times more browns than any other colour.'

'Are the brown bricks cheaper to make?'

'No. All our bricks cost the same to make. Colour don't matter.'

'Oh. So why do you make and sell more brown ones? Is brown a popular colour?'

'I doubt it, but' he said, screwing up his face, 'there's no accounting for taste.'

'I don't follow you. Why do you make more brown bricks? I mean, how can you tell that builders will prefer your brown bricks to, say, your white ones?'

'The browns are half the price of t'other colours!' he said still without a smile.

Things were beginning to look up. When Trevor told one or two business associates that he had switched from ICI to H & J Chemical Distributors Ltd, they followed suit. Impressed by Harry's prices and his prompt delivery service, they recommended him to people they knew. The business was growing. Work had started on the house next door or, as Joy named it, the *Millstone*. The concrete footings were laid. The bricks, sand and cement had been delivered. The cement mixer had been hired and delivered. Everything was ready and waiting for the bricklayers.

Monday came and went. Tuesday came and went. On Wednesday morning as a result of Harry's phone calls on the previous two days, the bricklayers appeared – *the gang of three* – as Joy called them. They were still drinking the cups of tea that Joy provided when Harry left for his *Kampf in dem Stalag* (his struggle for survival in the POW camp) as he called his work in the building he had renovated.

The gang's senior member, a short, stocky, weather-beaten man in his mid-fifties, had started up the *empty* mixer to disturb the normally quiet cul-de-sac with its noisy chugging. Harry would have driven away a happier man if, *before* taking the first of their many breaks, they had put some cement, sand and water in the mixer so the mortar would be ready when they finished their tea. What a useless bunch! Luckily they were being paid for the job and not by the hour. When Harry returned home that evening, Joy handed him a large sherry as he stepped inside the door and said ominously, 'I think you should inspect the bricklayers work.'

'What in heaven's name...' said Harry. 'They've... They've...'

'It's not right, is it?' said Joy.

'How could anybody be so stupid? I mean...'

'I did wonder what they were doing when I took them their mid-morning coffee.'

'Did you say anything to the guy in charge?'

'Yes. I asked Doug… that's their chargehand's name… I asked him about it.'

'What did he say?'

'He said he thought it a bit odd but told me they were 'spot on' according to the plans.'

'Good morning Dr Procter. Looks like it's going to be another nice day,' said Doug.

'Only as far as the weather is concerned. You'd better take a look over here at the wall you've built.' Harry led him to the far end of the side wall, which was already about five feet high. Pointing to the base, Harry said, 'Notice anything odd about this wall, Doug?'

'Can't say I do, sir. Good bit of brick laying, is that.' said Doug.

'Take a close look… right down here at the bottom. See anything wrong?'

'D' you mean with the bricks we used, sir?'

'No. They're fine. They're engineering bricks just as they should be.'

'Ah, that's OK then. You gave me a bit of a turn, you did, sir,' said Doug.

'No, look at the bottom… the first course of bricks. Look at the last thirty inches of this side wall and all along this back wall,' said Harry in quiet voice. 'What are they on?'

'Ah, now I'm with you, sir. As I told your good lady wife this morning, I thought it a bit odd but we had to stick to your plans.'

'A *bit odd*!' Harry hissed. 'You thought it a bit odd. You had to stick to my plans! Good God, man, you've gone beyond the concrete footings and built the wall on the soft soil!'

As a scientist, Harry was used to dealing with varying units of measurement; so he took Metrication and the 1959 international definition of the yard as 0.9144 metres in his stride. It was another matter for bricklayers and carpenters; they had a different stride. Harry saw that now. The crew laying the footings for the side wall saw 12 on the plan as yards (36 feet). The *gang of three* saw 12 on the plan as metres (39.37 feet). Harry was too distraught to see the funny side of it when Doug said to him, 'Our brickwork is *spot on*, Dr Procter. It's them footings; they're *short*.'

H & J Chemicals kept Harry so busy that it was up to Joy to keep a weather eye on the tradesmen. She did her best. Each morning before he left for work Harry would give her a note of points to watch for. Each evening when he came home he would carefully check on progress. Progress was slower than they had originally hoped but, in the light of their experience, it was proving better than they might have expected. All too often life's problems are the unexpected.

'This takes the biscuit,' said Harry to himself. 'Joy! Come up here and see this.'

'What now?' said Joy coming up the stairs of the *Millstone*.

The stairs ran straight up, from the small hallway just inside the front door, to a narrow landing, at right angles to the staircase. Directly at the head of the stairs was the doorway into a small shower room. The inward-opening door was half open. Inside and to the left of the door was the toilet. Inside and against the wall facing the doorway was the hand washbasin. Inside and to the right, out of sight behind the door was the shower cubicle.

'The latest lunacy, that's what,' said Harry. 'Take a look inside the shower room.'

'What am I looking for?' asked Joy, nervously.

'You'll see. Just step inside.'

'The toilet looks fine,' said Joy. 'Oh, there's no toilet seat. Is that it?'

26

'No. The plumber will probably fit the seat and the cover tomorrow. Carry on.'

'The hand washbasin looks… Oh!' said Joy, as the door bumped against the edge of the washbasin. 'Is that supposed to happen?'

'No. It shouldn't. The plumber will have to move the basin a bit to the right for the door to clear it,' said Harry. 'Carry on. Take a look at the shower cubicle.'

'How am I supposed to do that?' said Joy. 'Peer around the door?'

'Of course not,' said Harry, a grin appearing on his face. 'You'll have to step inside and close the door.'

'Is this a joke?' Joy exclaimed. She had stepped into the corner of the room and tried to shut the door; it bumped against the toilet basin. 'The door's trapped between the washbasin and loo. It won't open and it won't shut!'

'Well spotted. Any thoughts?'

'Yes. We must be as crazy to have started this house as the tradesmen who are building it. How could anybody be so stupid?'

When Harry started laughing, Joy saw the funny side of it and started laughing too. They were learning the hard way that people need to communicate and cooperate. How did that shower room door come to be stuck between the hand washbasin and the toilet?

According to Harry, the plumber fixed the washbasin to the wall.

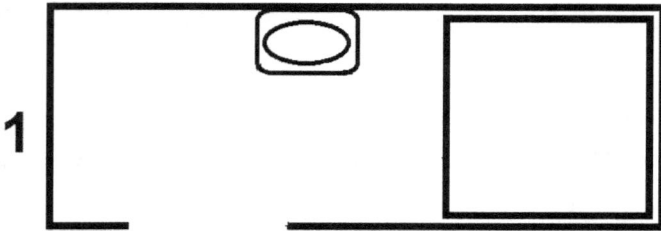

The carpenter hung the door.

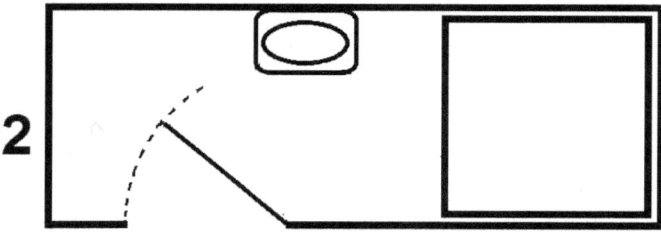

Then the plumber pushed open the door, fixed the toilet basin to the floor.

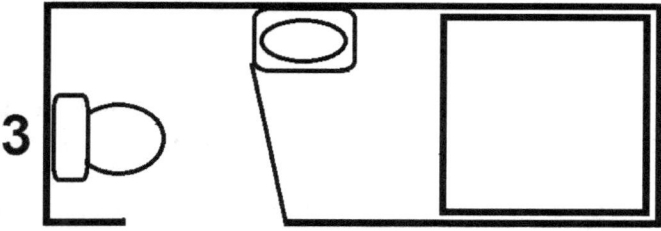

The plumber left the door open and the site foreman did not check their work.

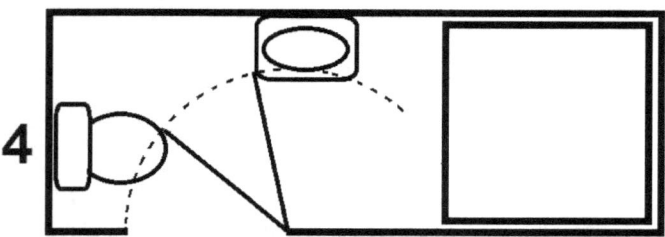

The *Millstone* was sold, the profit deposited in the bank and the ground rent was added monthly to the company's account. H & J

Builders Ltd contracted tradesmen to renovate two more buildings on the old POW camp site and Harry hired Tom Matthews, a recently retired HG Chemicals laboratory technician, to help part-time in their steadily expanding Chemical Distribution business.

Using the time he once devoted to caring for his lawn, Harold Procter, B.Sc. Ph.D. wrote and published a book on the theory and practical applications of ion exchange and spent the modest royalties on the occasional bottle of sherry and on his wine making. Things were looking up. The future looked bright. But as the Buddhist saying goes *the unexpected is bound to happen; the anticipated never comes.*

* * * * *

The four deck chairs faced the river. The two men wore straw hats to shield their heads from the warm Sunday afternoon sun. Dot and Joy had gone indoors to make a cup of tea. Jonathon, Harry's only son, had gone for a cycle ride with Susan and Jennifer, Trevor's two daughters.

'Six across, eight letters,' said Harry, '*torpid company precedes mother's twisted toes.*' Trevor never understood how anybody could spend any time on crosswords, especially the cryptic crossword in the Telegraph. 'Company… that'll be co. Mother is probably ma… toes… that's an anagram,' said Harry, encouragingly. We're looking for another word for torpid.' Trevor remained silent. Just then the two ladies arrived with the teas and slices of Dutch orange cake that Joy had baked that morning. 'You'd better grab a piece of cake before the kids get back, Trevor. You know what gannets they are.'

'Have you been at my crossword again, Dr Procter?' said Joy.

'Oh, it's yours, is it?' said Trevor. 'I thought it was Harry's.'

'I was just reading Trevor an easy clue to stop him being torpid and lethargic.'

'Six across, eight letters,' said Trevor. 'A word meaning torpid according to Harry.'

'Comatose,' said Joy, after a quick glance.

'Being in a coma,' muttered Dot under her breath.

'Sounds like the kids are back,' said Harry. 'Better grab your piece of cake, Trevor.'

The four adults settled into their deck chairs to enjoy their quiet cup of tea in the garden at the back of the house. At the front of the house, Jonathon, Susan and Jennifer, put the bikes in the garage. Jonathon wanted to go straight indoors to get an ice-cream from the 'fridge but Susan said they should first tell their parents they were back. So, Jonathon followed Susan to the path at the side of the house. Jennifer, the younger sister, trailed along behind them.

Joy was listening to their faint footsteps when suddenly there was a deafening noise, the sound of metal crashing to the ground, as though a bomb had gone off, and almost simultaneously a loud scream. Then just as suddenly there was silence, broken only by the whispered gurgling of the Stour river flowing gently and unceasingly past the bottom of the garden.

Harry was first on the scene with Trevor close on his heels; their two wives were not far behind, with Dorothy slightly ahead of Joy. Both men had occasionally rendered first aid to their colleagues injured in minor accidents at work. They now had something quite different to deal with. Jonathon was lying on the path, on his back, with Susan, her head and face covered in blood, lying crumpled across his legs. Jennifer, her face ashen, her body shaking, her hands over her ears was staring down at the two seemingly motionless bodies. Suddenly she became hysterical and started to scream. Along the path and lying across Jonathon's left arm and Jennifer's left leg was a long length of cast iron guttering.

'What's happened?' said Joy, looking over Dot's shoulder.'

'An accident,' said Dot calmly. 'Trevor, take Joy and Jennifer indoors. Harry! You phone for an ambulance then get back here as quick as you can with a blanket and cushions.'

'My God!' screamed Joy, losing her usual composure. 'Jonathon! Jonathon!'

'Come on old girl,' said Trevor, 'help me get Jennifer indoors. She'll need a cup of tea.'

Before she met Trevor, Dorothy had worked as a State Registered Nurse (SRN) and done a stint in the emergency ward of the local hospital. When she checked her daughter and found no pulse or any other signs of life, Dorothy showed no outward signs of emotion. Grief was for later. During the short time that Harry was gone, she forced herself not to look at or think about her daughter Susan who was dead but to concentrate on Jonathon who was alive albeit only just.

As soon as Harry came back, Dorothy got him to help her gently lift Susan's body off Jonathon and put cushions underneath his legs to raise them ten inches off the ground (to improve blood flow to the brain) and to cover his body with the blanket (to keep him warm and improve his circulation). His breathing was rapid and shallow; his pulse was fast and weak but there was no sign of bleeding where the heavy cast iron had struck Jonathon on the head.

Harry and Dorothy waited until the ambulance had left before they went indoors to join the others. 'Jennifer,' said Dorothy Partridge, SRN, hugging her daughter, 'I want you to be brave.' Jennifer had stopped shaking and the colour had returned to her cheeks. 'I want you to be very brave.' Jennifer nodded dumbly and raised her eyes to see a look on her mother's face that she had never seen before. 'Susan and Jonathon have been taken to hospital.'

* * * * *

It rained all day. Black clouds filled the sky and it was still raining in the late afternoon when everybody except Harry and Joy had gone home. Jennifer had gone to her room as soon as they had returned from the crematorium. Joy helped Dot with the washing up in the kitchen. Harry helped Trevor tidy the dining room. When they could find nothing else to occupy their hands, the four friends sat quietly together in the lounge.

The vicar of the local church, where Susan had been a loyal member of the choir, had conducted the service with sensitivity and sincerity, exuding a genuine faith that enabled Trevor and Dorothy to take comfort from his reading of the words

> *I am the resurrection and the life,' saith the*
> *Lord; 'he that believeth in me, though he*
> *were dead, yet shall he live: and whosoever*
> *liveth and believeth in me shall never die.*

But when he began *We therefore commit her body to the ground; earth to earth, ashes to ashes, dust to dust...* and the coffin began to move slowly out of sight, Dorothy could no longer hold back her tears. She was not alone in her expression of grief.

'I fancy a cup of tea?' said Trevor, breaking the silence and starting to get up. 'Anybody else?'

'I won't say no,' said Harry.

'You sit down,' said Dot, 'I'll make it. You fancy a cup, Joy?'

'Yes, that would be nice, Dot, but we must be going soon,' Joy said, glancing at Harry. 'I'll come and give you a hand.'

'Look here, Harry,' Trevor said, staring solemnly at his friend, 'you must stop blaming yourself. It was an accident pure and simple.'

'It was not,' said Harry quietly, 'an unforeseen event without an apparent cause, Trevor. The cause was those rusty iron brackets failing to hold up that cast iron gutter. I should have foreseen that. My God, Jennifer could have been killed as well.'

'Well, we must thank God that she wasn't. What's the latest news on Jonathon?' Before Harry could reply, Dorothy and Joy came in with the tea.

At the front door, the women hugged one another, then Harry hugged Dot and Trevor hugged Joy. As he gripped Harry's right hand and put his left hand on his friend's shoulder, Trevor whispered into his ear, 'We don't blame you, old man. Please, for our sake, don't blame yourself.'

* * * * *

'Rest assured, Mrs Procter, we are doing all we can for your son. It was fortunate that there was an experienced nurse on hand at the time of the accident. She almost certainly saved his life.'

'I must apologize for my husband's outburst, doctor. He's very worried... we both are.'

'That's alright. I quite understand but he was quite correct when he said that someone who has suffered mild TBI usually becomes conscious within thirty minutes.'

'We're worried because Jonathon has been unconscious for nearly a week. My husband thinks the traumatic brain injury is severe and that Jonathon is at risk from secondary injuries caused by intracranial pressure.'

'As I tried to tell Dr Procter, there's been no sign of mydriasis or papilloedema.'

'I'm sorry, doctor, my husband may have understood you but...'

'Ah, yes, I'm sorry. Mydriasis is an excessive dilation of the pupils, one of the symptoms of severe TBI. Papilloedema is swelling of the optic disc, one of the indicators of increased intracranial pressure, a major cause of secondary brain injury. Look Mrs Procter, I know it's easier for me to say than it is for you, Jonathon's mother, to do... but please try not to worry. Your son is in good hands.'

Joy spent as much time at Jonathon's bedside as the hospital would allow. She held his hand, stroked his hair, read to him and played him his favourite music. Harry had to spend his days mixing and delivering chemicals but he spent his evenings at the hospital. Joy remained optimistic. Harry remained pessimistic, disparaging the medical science as nothing more than the art of ascribing fancy labels to sets of symptoms. He was beginning to wear Joy down.

'You're getting on my nerves,' Joy snapped. 'I wish you could go outside and mow your precious lawn,' The moment she said that she regretted it. Harry scowled, stormed out of the house and marched down the back lanes and across the fields to the Bull Inn. By the time he got there, he had calmed down. Outside in the warm sunshine, he sat on a wooden bench to sip a half pint of cider and gather his thoughts.

Jonathon was alive, albeit still unconscious, and there was nothing that he, Dr Harry Procter, could do to alter that fact. Joy was worried stiff about Jonathon and the strain was beginning to show and he wasn't helping. There was something he could and would do about that. His lawn was a distant memory; he must forget it. That piece of cast iron gutter was still lying at the side of the house; he should deal with that. 'Why on earth didn't I check and replace those rusty brackets?' Harry said under his breath. And then another thought struck him. 'Why on earth do we still use cast iron guttering? Why don't we use PVC gutters?'

* * * * *

'I didn't realize there was such a pretty walk to the Bull Inn,' said Joy. 'When did you discover it?'

'This morning,' said Harry, helping Joy over a style and taking hold of her hand again. 'Look I'm sorry I've been so thoughtless and upsetting you lately. I...'

'That's alright, Harry, I know,' she said, squeezing his hand. 'It's Jonathon. We're both worried.'

'It's my fault, I...'

'Once and for all, Harry Procter, it's not your fault. You're always telling me that what's done is done and can't be undone? It's about time you began practising what you preach.'

'You're right. Of course you're right. The brackets rusted and the cast iron guttering killed Jenny and nearly killed Jonathon. I can't undo that *but* I'll make absolutely sure it never happens again.'

After a cheese and pickle lunch at the Bull Inn, Harry walked Joy home along a different path, part of which was thought to date back to Roman times. They passed a derelict water mill built in the late 18th century on the site where, Harry supposed, the Romans might have built a water mill to grind corn. The pub lunch and the walk together in the fresh air were just what they needed.

Harry held Joy's interest and kept her mind off the problems with his knowledge of local history and plant chemistry. 'The yew is evergreen and a good shrub for hedges. Its attractive scarlet berries are harmless but the seeds inside and the shrub's needle-like leaves contain a deadly poison; one of a group of compounds we call alkaloids,' said Harry. 'The caffeine in your coffee is an alkaloid.'

As they turned the corner into their cul-de-sac, Harry said, "I found out the other day that during the Second World War the German prisoners built their own camp where we've got H & J Chemicals and that the Luftwaffe strafed the camp twice thinking it was a munitions factory. After the war, a lot of the prisoners married local girls and stayed in England. There's a rumour that Merck, a German Corporation, is planning to take over HG Chemicals. Ironic! The Jerrys couldn't beat us so they're joining us.'

'I really enjoyed that little outing, Harry,' said Joy when they were back home in their sitting room drinking a cup of tea. 'You made it very interesting. We ought to do it again sometime and take Dot and Trevor with us.'

'You've just given me my second idea today,' said Harry.

'I've seen that look on your face all too often lately, Dr Procter,' Joy said. 'What now?'

'We're going to walk to a different pub each weekend. You can take notes or record what I say and we'll publish a book. We'll call it Sunday Pub Walks.'

'That was the idea I gave you? What was the other idea you've had?'

'To form another company,' said Harry. 'H & J Plastics Ltd.'

35

'Why? What on earth for?'

'To replace every heavy, rusty iron gutter and bracket with light, rustproof PVC ones.'

Harry was familiar with the plastic PolyVinylChloride. It was a rigid and strong polymer. It was cheap to produce and easily extruded into various shapes, like pipes and gutters, that would be five or six times lighter than their cast iron equivalent. PVC is white but it can be coloured grey; it does not discolour or deteriorate when exposed to the elements. What Harry couldn't understand was why PVC downpipes and gutters had not already replaced cast iron ones. He soon found out why they hadn't.

'So what you're saying is this,' said Trevor, 'some companies have produced PVC pipes and gutters but haven't worked out an economical way to assemble them?'

'That's about it,' said Harry. 'When cast iron replaced lead for gutters and pipes early in the nineteenth century, the joints between the sections were filled with plumbers putty and bolted together.'

'That didn't always stop the leaks though,' said Trevor. 'Putty goes brittle and cracks after a while. Have they tried using putty with plastic gutters and pipes?'

'That's probably what they tried first. They've experimented with various adhesives but with limited success. In my opinion, we've got to stop treating PVC as just a replacement for cast iron. I think I might have a solution to the problem.'

* * * * *

For almost four weeks, Jonathon remained in a coma and Joy would not even think about forming another company; her son was her priority. Meanwhile, using whatever spare time he could generate during the day, Harry converted a small building into a workshop on their company site; he still spent his evenings at the hospital and took Joy, with her pocket recorder, on a guided walk each Sunday for lunch at a different pub. It was the Tuesday after their fourth pub walk that Joy called Harry from the hospital.

36

'Harry,' she said between sobs, 'Jonathon's... Jonathon's... He's...'

'Joy?' said Harry, trying to keep the panic out of his voice. 'What's happened?'

Since his first emotional encounter with the consultant in charge of Jonathon's case, Harry had performed an extensive search of the medical journals and was now prepared to concede that there was a little more to medical science than just applying labels to symptoms.

There was no doubt that his son had suffered a closed head injury (CHI); he had undoubtedly been struck on the head by an object that did not break the skull. There was also little doubt that his son had suffered, to use the medical jargon, a traumatically induced physiologic disruption of brain function (TBI) manifested by a period of loss of consciousness (LOC); he had undoubtedly been unconscious for a worryingly long time.

What was in doubt was the severity of the injury and the extent to which it might lead to permanent or temporary impairment of cognitive, physical, and psychosocial functions, with an associated diminished or altered state of consciousness, to quote yet more jargon. This doubt was going around in Harry's head when he found Joy, her eyes still red-rimmed, smiling and talking to the doctor in the hospital corridor.

'Ah, Dr Procter, there you are,' said the senior consultant. 'Your son Jonathon regained consciousness this afternoon and is in a responsive state. His rude awakening, if I may call it that, gave your wife a bit of a scare.'

'He frightened the life out of me Harry. Luckily a nurse was with me at the time.'

'Moaning and thrashing around, was he?' said Harry.

'And a terrible look on his face,' said Joy. 'I thought he was having a seizure.'

'As I was just explaining to Mrs Procter,' said the consultant, gripping the lapel of his white coat with his left hand and putting his right hand into its pocket, 'recovery in real life is rather different from that portrayed in TV medical soap opera, as you yourself obviously know.'

'How responsive is Jonathon?' asked Harry.

'So far he has responded to hearing, sight and touch but it's rather early...'

'to expect him to say anything that makes sense?' interrupted Harry.

'Yes, a bit too early to say but I'm hopeful that there's been little or no damage to either the frontal or the parietal regions. I expect you'd like to see him now, so if you'll excuse me, Dr Procter... Mrs Procter... I'm wanted in theatre.'

Jonathon turned his head towards the door when Joy and Harry walked into the room and over to his bed. His eyes were open but there was no expression on his face. Joy sat down on her usual chair, smiled at Jonathon and smoothed back his hair. Harry pulled up a chair and sat down beside Joy.

When Harry said *how are you, Jonathon*, he saw his son turn his head towards him. When he put his hand under his son's left hand, he felt Jonathon grip it tightly. Then Joy started saying how worried they had been; how happy they were now that he was awake; how everything was going to be alright. Harry noted that Jonathon turned his head towards Joy but still with what seemed a blank look.

'See you this evening, son,' said Harry, letting go of Jonathon's hand and standing up. 'Can I bring you anything?' His son's head moved slowly from side to side.

'I'll stay here,' said Joy. 'When you come back we can get something to eat in the hospital cafeteria, if you don't mind.'

'Fine by me,' said Harry, smiling and waving to his son. 'I'll be back as soon as I can.'

* * * * *

'Hello, son,' said Harry. 'Your mother will be here in a minute. How are you doing? OK?' Jonathon had turned his head towards Harry but there was still no expression on his face. 'I've got two liquids for you to smell. Tell me what they are, OK?' Harry took the lid off a tiny glass bottle of iso-amyl acetate and held it near his son's nose; the strong odour of pear drops caused no change in Jonathon's facial expression. Then Harry held his breath and took the lid off a tiny bottle containing just one drop of butanethiol, held it briefly under his son's nose then quickly replaced the lid. At that precise moment Joy walked into the room and saw Jonathon's face screwed up in a look of disgust.

'My God, Harry, what's that awful smell?'

'Butyl mercaptan,' said Harry smiling broadly. 'Better known as *skunk's spray*.'

'It's utterly revolting. Where's it from, if I really need to ask?'

'From H & J Chemicals. Butyl mercaptan or butanethiol, to give it its proper chemical name, is one of the industrial solvents we supply to the gas board.'

'Why on earth do they want that? It smells horrible.'

'That's the point. Our human noses can detect the smell when there's as little as 10 parts of butanethiol in 1 billion parts of air. They add it to the natural gas supply so we can detect gas leaks; methane – natural gas to you - is odourless.'

'And you brought that stuff here because…?'

'I wanted to see Jonathon's reaction.'

'I think I saw that. He looked…'

'Precisely! I'm delighted to say he looked disgusted,' said Harry. 'Now don't get your hopes up. It's just one simple response test and it's not in the medical books; but it suggests that his frontal lobes may not be damaged.'

'Oh! Hello!' said Harry when the nurse walked in and he saw the look on her face. 'Sorry about the smell. There hasn't been a gas leak. I was just...'

'The smell will soon go,' said Joy turning to the nurse. 'It's nothing to worry about.'

* * * * *

When he walked into his son's hospital room the following evening, Jonathon was sitting up in bed and looking more alert. Harry had two more tiny bottles of liquids; this time for Jonathon to taste. The dilute sugar solution produced no reaction but his son screwed up his face at the dilute acetic acid solution. Harry noted the response and explained to Joy that one of the results of frontal lobe damage is loss of sense of smell and/or taste. What he didn't tell her was that frontal lobe damage can affect speech.

On Friday, at Harry's suggestion, Joy took her Telegraph crossword to the hospital and read the clues to Jonathon who had still not spoken since he regained consciousness on Tuesday. Her son nodded when she asked if he would like to help her. There was no other response from him until Joy read out, '12 across... six letters... *murky after a street that smells*,' and said, 'st for street are the first two letters then...' Jonathon made a noise.

That evening Joy couldn't in all honesty tell Harry that their son had spoken intelligibly but she believed with all her heart that he was trying to say *stinky*. Neither could she say that *stinky* was a secret nickname she and Jonathon had for Harry when he brought his laboratory coat home from work for her to wash.

* * * * *

In the first few months following the tragic accident, Joy played little part in company business; she devoted herself to Jonathon's rehabilitation. Tom Matthews, now full-time, handled their chemical distribution business so that Harry could spend most of his time in solitary confinement in his workshop.

One Sunday, early in the evening, Joy walked into Dot's kitchen where her friend was making a cup of tea. Before she could start on as usual about Jonathon's progress and ask Dot her professional opinion - as a qualified nurse and not just as a friend, Dot said, 'Is everything alright with you and Harry?'

'What do you mean?' said Joy.

'You know,' said Dot. 'Is everything OK between you two?'

'Why do you ask?'

'Well, to be honest, you're not…'

'What?' snapped Joy, 'I'm not what?'

'There! You see,' said Dot. 'The Joy I once knew wouldn't have done that.'

'Done what?'

'Bitten my head off before I finished saying you're not your old self. As for Harry… well Trevor thinks…'

'What about Harry? What does Trevor think?'

'There you go again, Joy.' Dot said quietly. 'Sit down and drink your tea. I'll take the tray to the others in the sitting room and come straight back.'

The two friends sat facing one another across the small kitchen table and talked. Actually Joy talked and Dot listened. 'I'm sorry. You're right. I've not been myself since…' Dot waited while Joy wiped her eyes and blew her nose. 'I seem to be the only one worried about our Jonathon. Harry leaves the house early, often without waiting to have breakfast with us; and he often comes home too late to eat supper with us. I think I told you that I have been going on bike rides with Jonathon.' Dot nodded.

41

'Well. One day we cycled to the building where Jonathon used to help mix the acids,' continued Joy. 'Harry wasn't in there. Tom... you know, Harry's part-time assistant... used to work at HG Chemicals... Tom told us that Harry was in his workshop. Well anyway, we went to the workshop but Harry wouldn't let us in to see what he was doing. When he came home that evening and I asked him again what he was doing, he said he was sorry but he couldn't talk about it to anyone, not even me.' Dot sipped her tea. 'We never had secrets from one another and dealing with those cowboys building the house next door... that taught us a lesson... at least I thought it did... about the importance of communicating.'

Dr Harold Procter no longer had analytical chemistry, wine making and lawn care as his hobbies which Joy had called his three obsessions. He now had just one obsession - Joy might have called it a hobby - that was his obsession with the problem of PVC gutters.

'Trevor thinks that Harry is working too hard,' said Dot.

'Trevor's probably right. It's just that... well I don't know what's got into him.'

'If Harry says he can't talk about what he's doing in that workshop, then I'm sure he'll have a very good reason. And stop worrying so much about Jonathon. He's doing very well. You'll see a big difference when he starts back to school after the holidays. By the way, we want the three of you to slum it and come to us for lunch on Christmas day.'

Jonathon helped Jennifer lay the table. Joy helped Dot bring in the food from the kitchen. Trevor carved the turkey. Harry poured the wine. Dot helped everybody to the meat, sage & onion stuffing and cranberry sauce. Everybody helped themselves to roast potatoes, roast parsnips, carrots, peas and Brussel sprouts. Trevor gave thanks for what they were about receive. They pulled their crackers, put on their paper hats and tucked into the traditional Christmas Day fare.

Joy had insisted on making the plum pudding and the brandy sauce. When Trevor pretended he'd just broken a tooth on a sixpence, everybody laughed as Joy rose to the bait. 'There are no coins in my pudding, Trevor Partridge. An awful idea dreamed up by Queen Victoria's Prince Albert when he introduced Britain to his German plum pudding.' When the men had done the washing up and they had all listened to the Queen's speech on the radio, the two families went for a walk together.

'Harry takes us for a walk on Sunday when the weather's fine. I don't suppose you'd like to join us?'

'I would,' said Trevor, 'but I can't speak for these two. When do you start?'

'We usually leave the house at about half past ten and drive to the pub…'

'I thought you said he takes you for a *walk*?' said Trevor.

'That's right. We start the walk at a pub and get back there in time for a pub lunch. The walk usually takes about an hour to an hour and a half.'

'Now *that* sounds like my kind of walk,' said Trevor.

'What about church?' said Dot.

'Ah, yes, church. We usually go to the eleven o'clock service. Oh well, we'll just have to get up earlier and attend the nine o'clock,' said Trevor, shrugging his shoulders.

Trevor and Dot spent the evening at Harry and Joy's house while Jonathon went with Jennifer to a friend's party to see in the New Year. As midnight struck, Trevor raised his glass and wished them all good health, happiness and prosperity. As they linked hands in friendship for *Auld Lang Syne*, Trevor and Dorothy sorrowed for the daughter they had lost; Joy worried about the son she still had and Harry was trying to decide if he should trust his wife and Trevor.

In the months since the accident, Harry had worked secretly in his workshop to solve the PVC gutter problem. It took less than two weeks to produce a solution *on paper*. It took much longer to get his solution off the drawing board and to produce a prototype. His idea was simple enough. Seal the joint, between two lengths of PVC

43

gutter, with a strip of synthetic rubber and hold the joint tightly together with a clip that would also fix the gutter to the fascia board.

The difficulty was designing a clip that was strong enough to support the gutter but just flexible enough for the gutter to be pressed down into the clip.

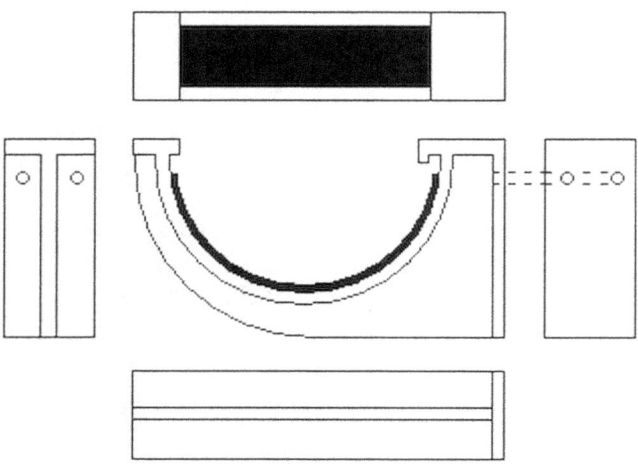

Harry lost count of the number of times he went 'back to the drawing board.' It was the morning of New Year's Eve when he locked the final plans and his precious prototype gutter bracket safely in his workshop. Joy and Trevor were still on his mind when he climbed into bed just after 1 a.m.

Harry slid out of bed just after 9 o'clock, crept downstairs to the kitchen and made a cup tea for himself and a coffee for his wife. While the tea was brewing, he tried to reassure himself that he had come to the right decision and had no other option.

'Hello Dot! Harry here. Is Trevor around?'

'Yes. Hang on a minute, I'll give him a shout,' said Dorothy putting her hand over the telephone mouthpiece.

'Hello old boy. What's up?'

'I need to speak to you, Trevor. Could you spare me an hour this afternoon?'

'Yes of course, old boy. It sounds serious. What's it all about?'

'You'll find out. I'll pop round to your place at two o'clock if that's alright.'

'See you at two, Harry.'

He tackled Joy that morning after breakfast. She listened patiently to what Harry had to say and agreed to go along with his proposals as long as Trevor didn't object.

'Harry's here,' Dot called out when she saw Harry's car pull up outside.

'Shan't be long, Dot,' said Trevor. 'We're just popping up the road.'

'I'll expect you when I see you, love,' said Dot waving to Harry through the kitchen window.

'Where are we going?' asked Trevor as he lowered his bulk into the passenger seat.

'I suppose you could say to prison,' said Harry not taking his eyes off the road.

'It's that serious then?'

'Oh yes,' said Harry.

'You're right,' said Trevor. 'This place has more security than Fort Knox.

'What do you know about patent law?' Harry asked, as he led Trevor into the workshop and securely locked the door behind them.

'Not nearly enough,' said Trevor. 'I know Dad took out the patents on some of his plating processes but he never talked about it. In fact he was secretive to the point of paranoia'

45

'I'm not surprised,' said Harry. 'As far as I can gather, if he had told anybody, then his inventions would not have been novel and therefore not patentable.'

'By *novel* you mean...?'

'Legal jargon for *new* to everybody except the applicant for the patent. If your dad told you about his invention *before* he applied for a patent, then strictly speaking it would not have been novel.'

'I see,' said Trevor, when he clearly didn't see.

Before bringing Trevor to the workshop, Harry had talked with Joy about forming a third company, H & J Plastics Ltd, and explained how and why he wanted to do it. He didn't tell Joy about his inventions in detail not because he couldn't trust her but because he didn't think she would be interested. Trevor was Harry's best friend and also somebody he could trust; even so, he wouldn't tell Trevor about his invention unless he had to.

'How long have we known one another, Trevor?'

'Let's see now. You and Joy were godparents to Susan Louise...'

'Eighteen years or thereabouts?' interrupted Harry.

'Yes, I'd say at least eighteen years. Why? What's on your mind?'

'Money for a start, Trevor. Quite a lot of money, as a matter of fact.'

'What's it for, old boy?'

'I'm not sure I should tell you.'

'I see,' said Trevor, when once again he clearly didn't. 'Just how much is *quite a lot*?'

'Ten thousand pounds to start with and anything up to two hundred thousand over the next four months.'

'That *is* quite a bit of money,' said Trevor with a whistle of surprise. 'You want a loan?'

'No. I don't want a loan. I want you to invest it in a plastics company.'

'What company?'

'H & T Plastics Ltd,' said Harry.

'Never heard of them, old boy.'

'I'm not surprised. We haven't formed the company yet,' said Harry.

'We meaning…?'

'You, me, Dot and Joy.'

'Has this got something to do with the bee in your bonnet about PVC gutters?'

'I'll answer that if you'll agree to be an equal partner in H & T Plastics Ltd.'

After the two men shook hands, Trevor listened patiently while Harry, without revealing any details of his designs and prototype, enthused about inexpensive, easy-to-install PVC guttering and downpipes not only to replace existing cast iron ones but also to install in all new housing. 'I haven't prepared a formal business plan. I'd like to leave that to you and Joy,' Harry said in reply to Trevor's question. 'Freddy York, our lawyer, will register our new company,' Harry said in reply to Trevor's second question. 'I'll be completing the rest of the designs and prototypes of the components so our company can apply for the patents,' he said when Trevor asked what he would be doing.

A month later, the four directors of the newly formed company, H & T Plastics Ltd, gathered in the workshop. Harry unlocked the safe, took out his prototype PVC bracket and showed his three partners how it would work. Trevor was impressed but Dot and Joy were less than enthusiastic.

'This is what's taken all your spare time, is it?' said Joy. 'What do you think of it Dot?'

'I don't know what to think, to be honest,' said Dot. 'Is this what our company's going to make, Harry?'

'Yes,' said Harry, 'but not just brackets. We're going to produce a complete rainwater system made from PVC.' And saying that, Harry showed them his plans for junctions to join gutters at roof corners and to seal gutters to down-pipes.

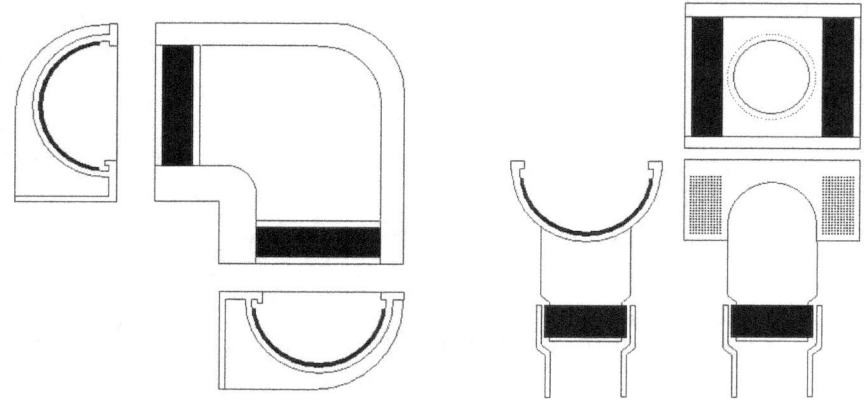

'What do you think of all this Trevor?' said Joy.

'It's a first class job. There's nothing like it on the market. It's a vast improvement on the cast iron guttering that...' He broke off when he saw the look on Dot's face.

'We've a long road ahead of us. I still have to make the prototypes for these junctions and apply for patents.'

'We've got to have the jigs, machinery and tools made,' said Trevor.

'And set up in a suitable factory,' said Harry.

'How much will all this cost and where are we going to get the money from?' said Joy.

'Quite a bit,' said Harry, 'and you'll probably have to work your charms on Thornton again.' He was right.

'How long is all this going to take?' said Dot.

'A few months if we're lucky,' said Trevor. 'but it could take two years for the patents.'

'Ah, but we don't have to wait that long,' said Harry. 'We can start production as soon as our patents are pending.'

'What do I tell Thornton when he asks what turnover we predict for the first three years?'

'One million pounds,' chorused Harry and Trevor. How wrong they were.

* * * * *

Over the next two years, whenever weather permitted, the Partridge and Procter families went on one of Harry's *Sunday Pub Walks*. Dot kept Joy company. Jennifer kept Jonathon company; he was still finding it difficult to be sociable. Trevor not only recorded what Harry said but also took photographs and asked pertinent questions.

Over those two years, as his way of escape from the pressures of business, Harry made time to publish three books of *Sunday Pub Walks* for which Trevor provided sketch maps of the walks. When Trevor refused Harry's offer of a share in the profit from the sales, Joy and Dot secretly arranged to pay the money into a trust fund for Jennifer's higher education. And in spite of his friend's objections, Harry always printed in the books his thanks to Trevor Partridge for the photographs and sketch maps.

'How old is The Crown Hotel?'

'There was probably a Crown Hotel here in Blandford as far back as the 13th century. But if you mean this building, Trevor' said Harry, 'then I'd guess it's about two hundred years old. It was probably built soon after the great fire of 1731; about the time they started making cast iron gutters.'

'Jonathon still doesn't remember...'

'No. He remembers coming back from the cycle ride but doesn't remember walking around the side of the house or being hit on the head,' said Harry.

'Changing the subject,' said Trevor, 'I still don't understand why it took nearly two years to get our patent certificates.'

'Well, for a start, the Patent Office had to do a search to decide whether our patent applications are, to use their jargon, new or obvious. That took nearly a year and wasn't cheap. They also did what they call substantive examinations of our applications to establish, for example, that someone with reasonable technical know-how could follow our descriptions and make what we are trying to patent.'

'But you never had any doubts about getting them, did you old boy?'

'No, not really. You see our inventions...'

'*Your* inventions, Harry, not ours...'

'No! *Our* inventions. Once and for all, Trevor, they belong to H & T Plastics Ltd.'

'You know what I mean, Harry. *You* invented the bracket and...'

'I know, I know. Let's not argue about it,' said Harry. 'Now, what was I saying?'

'Something about why you never had any doubts about getting the patent certificates.'

'Ah, yes. I never had any doubts because *our* inventions met the Patent Office's four crucial requirements. Our inventions were *functional* and *technical* because they related to how something works - what it does, what it is made of and how it is made. They were *novel* because we hadn't made them public in any way, anywhere in the world, before we applied for the patents.'

50

'So that's why you wouldn't show us your plans and prototypes until we'd formed the company,' said Trevor. 'I see… But you told Freddy York?'

'Yes,' said Harry nodding. 'and I told the patent agent Freddy recommended. The Patent Office regard those conversations as confidential.'

'I see,' said Trevor, when he obviously didn't.

'*Our* inventions also met the third and fourth requirements. They had inventive steps not obvious to someone with a good knowledge of gutters and downpipes. And, most important of all, especially where we're concerned, our inventions could be made and would have commercial and industrial uses.'

The two families ate their pub lunch at The Crown in a small private room that Joy had booked for the occasion. Trevor gave thanks for their blessings and for the food they were about to receive. Over their coffee at the end of the meal, they began counting their blessings. Joy proudly announced that Jonathon had passed his exams and was going to study chemistry at Bristol University.

Dot announced with equal pride that Jennifer, two years Jonathon's junior, had passed her exams and was going into the Sixth Form to study English, French and German. Harry quietly announced that H & T Plastics Ltd had finally received the certificates for all their patents and that the company was going to apply for US and European patents. When asked what he had to announce, Trevor stood slowly to his feet and with a solemn face dropped his bombshell.

'About two and a half years ago, I said *if we're lucky* it might take a couple of years to get those patents and a few months to get our factory up and running. Well, we weren't so lucky. It took just over two years to get the patent certificates. Never mind; we've got them now thanks to Harry. It took just over a year to start production at the factory and the capital outlay was far more than we expected. Never mind that. The bank lent us the money thanks to Joy who, if you remember, told the manager we predicted a turnover of one million pounds for the first three years. Dear old Thornton assumed, of course, that was an *annual* turnover. Never mind.

Now, according to Jim Watson, our accountant, it's almost standard practice for any new business to make a loss in the first three years. Two days ago, I had an informal meeting with Jim. As a result of that get together, I have to announce bad news I'm afraid.'

Trevor looked gloomily around the table at each face in turn. When finally his eyes met Dot's, he announced in the flattest voice he could manage, that H & T Plastics Ltd looked set to make a profit, *not* a loss. As his face broke into a grin, Dot punched his shoulder. Joy looked at Harry and they began to laugh. Jennifer and Jonathon smiled not because they really understood the implications of what Trevor had just said but simply because their parents seemed happy. When Joy asked how much profit, Trevor said, 'It's hard to say just now but I rather think Thornton Metcalfe is going to be rather upset.'

'Why?' asked Joy.

'Banks make their money from interest on loans,' said Trevor.

'Yes, I understand that" said Joy. 'So?'

'So, he won't like it when we pay off our loan after just three years instead of ten!'

'But we borrowed £250,000. Are you saying…'

'Let's not be hasty,' said Trevor. 'Jim Watson's going to prepare a provisional set of accounts next week. All I'm saying now is that our business is looking up.'

'I wonder,' said Dot, 'where we'll be ten years from now?'

* * * * *

'Colonel Jeffreys is putting the *Millstone* up for auction, Harry'

'Oh, when did Monty tell you that?'

52

'He didn't. I just saw them putting up a board at the front,' said Joy. 'It was so sad, his wife dying suddenly like that. It was a heart attack apparently. She loved that house you know. I can't believe they've been living there for what, ten, no, nearly eleven years.'

'It must be worth ten times what they paid us for it,' said Harry. 'I wonder who'll buy it.'

'Yes, I wonder,' said Joy.

'Lot 14, ladies and gentlemen, is a well-appointed detached residence overlooking the Stour river. The large lounge and the fully fitted kitchen look out onto the garden and well maintained lawn at the rear. Upstairs there is a shower room and four bedrooms, two of which have bathrooms en suite. There is a two-car garage and hard standing for two more cars. Who will start the bidding at twelve thousand pounds?'

The auctioneer glanced around the room and saw a dealer nod. 'Twelve thousand pounds I'm bid. Any advance on twelve thousand.' Another dealer joined in with a bid of £12,500. 'Thank you,' said the auctioneer, 'twelve thousand five hundred I'm bid.' Several more dealers nodded and the bidding reached £14,500. 'Fourteen thousand five hundred I'm bid. Any advance on fourteen thousand five hundred?'

All the dealers, except the last one to bid, shook their heads; they knew the housing market and their limit had been reached. '£14,500 once, £14,500 twice…' A slender hand was raised. 'Thank you madam. Fifteen thousand pounds I'm bid. Any advance on £15,000? Going once. Going twice. Sold to the lady at the back of the room.'

'The four friends lay on upholstered sun-loungers by the pool of the Majestic Barrière, the luxury hotel on the world famous promenade, La Croisette.

'Is this your first visit to Cannes, Trevor?'

'Oh no, Dot and I come here every year for the film festival. Come off it Harry, you know full well this is the first time I've ever been to France.'

'He wouldn't be here now if Jennifer hadn't arranged it for us,' said Dot.

'Our Jennifer might have arranged it but we're paying for it and through the nose I might add. Ouch! What was that for?' said Trevor when Dot punched his bare shoulder.

'She likes working for Thomas Cook Travel Agency then?' said Harry.

'Loves it,' said Trevor, 'and they love her apparently.'

'Jennifer was disappointed that Jonathon couldn't come,' said Dot.

'Is she still sweet on him?' said Joy.

'As far as I know, they're still just very good friends but you can never tell what the future has in store, can you?' said Dot.

'Well I think it's safe to say that Jonathon is going to have a full-time job running our chemical distribution business,' said Harry. 'Other than that, I think you're right, Dot. You can never tell what's around the corner. And why, may I ask, are you looking at me like that, Mrs Joy Procter?'

'Oh, just wondering what the future's got in store for you, Dr Harry Procter.'

With Jennifer's help, Dot and Joy had played safe; they had booked a two-week stay at the hotel. During that time, Jonathon looked after H & J Chemical Distributors Ltd and also kept an eye on the work in progress on the *Millstone*. As Trevor turned his car into the cul-de-sac where the Procters lived, Joy's eyes fixed on Harry sitting in the front passenger seat.

'What the…' exclaimed Harry, as they approached their house.

'Problem, old man?' said Trevor.

'The *Millstone*! It's… It's gone!'

'Well blow me down,' said Trevor. 'So it has.' And then with a big grin on his face, he said, 'You'll soon get rid of that fat you put on these past two weeks.'

'What are you talking about?' said Harry.

'I'm talking about the work you're going to be doing; preparing the ground, fetching and sowing the seed and restoring your lawn to its former glory.

Two summers later, the two families were standing in the middle of the new lawn around a rose bush which Harry had planted with Trevor's help. The day was the day when, fifteen years previously, the accident had occurred that changed their lives; the rose bush was planted near the spot where Susan Louise Partridge had died.

As he stood looking at the profusion of light pink roses with their delicate fragrance, Harry was engulfed by a feeling of melancholy and guilt. He was still blaming himself for Susan's untimely death. When Joy held his arm, he was comforted by the fact that cast iron gutters and downpipes were becoming a thing of the past, that the hospital, where Jonathon had been a comatose patient, would soon be getting an MRI scanner, courtesy of H & T Plastics Ltd, and that Jennifer was going to marry Jonathon and help extend the chemical distribution business to Europe.

It was Dot who interrupted his thoughts. 'I don't know about anybody else,' she said, linking arms with her husband, 'but I'm ready for a cup of tea and a slice of Joy's cake.' As the group moved off, the sun lit up the metal plate at the base of the bush.

Species: Hybrid-T rose
Breeder: George E. Adams
Registered: 1929 America
Name: *Susan Louise*

---

* * * * *

55

Epilogue

The story I have told is a fiction based upon facts that were personally reported to me and events that I experienced firsthand. For instance, I knew a chemist, who left a major chemical company, solved a pollution problem, published a book of walks to unusual places, brewed his own wine and who, inspired by the fall of a cast iron gutter that might have killed his son, made his fortune in PVC guttering and downpipes.

We withdrew from a house being built when we saw, amongst other follies, the door trapped between the washbasin and toilet of the shower room. My neighbour called me to witness that the wall of his new house had been laid beyond the concrete footings. The owner of the local yard revealed to me his brick pricing secret. The Stour still runs through Dorset, UK.

Silver coins used to be put in Christmas puddings; if you found a silver sixpence in your portion, it was supposed to bring you good luck and you were supposed to make a wish; you were not supposed to break a tooth!

All that said, the names of the characters, the companies and the bank in the story are purely fictitious.

* * * * *

THE AXE MAN COMETH

On the 12th of December 1966, Frank Mitchell absconded from Her Majesty's prison high on Dartmoor in the English county of Devon. The following story is true and as accurate as my memory permits. I have not changed the names of the people involved, so I apologise in advance to those (living or dead) mentioned herein who might feel that I have portrayed them in a worse light than I portrayed myself.

* * * * *

In August 1966 my wife and I, together with our 2-year old daughter and 4-month old son, arrived at Thirlestaine Cottages in the grounds of Cheltenham College, the public school where I was to spend nearly five years teaching chemistry. Established in 1841, this independent private school was, during my time, only for boys, most of whom were boarders and fee-paying.

Thirlestaine House had sometime belonged to Lord Northwick and had housed an important collection of old masters (I refer to paintings and not schoolteachers). The College bought Thirlestaine, but not the paintings, in 1947 for use as a house for day-boys.

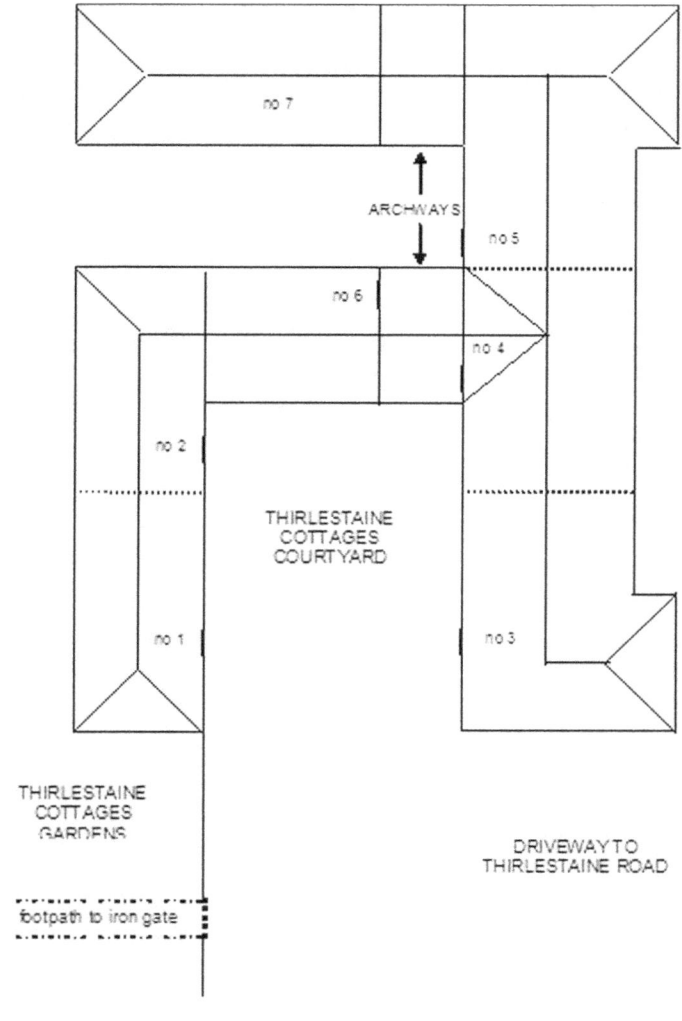

Cottage no. 1 was occupied by the secretary to the Bursar. Cottages 2, 3, 5, 6 and 7 were occupied by teaching staff. We moved into no. 4. cottage which had been vacated by Dr R C Whitfield, my predecessor in the chemistry department. The window of the lounge at the rear of the cottage looked onto a 200-year old cedar of Lebanon whose 78ft canopy sheltered a well-kept lawn.

Our front door – the only way in and out of the cottage – was within an archway. Diagonally opposite was the entrance to no. 6 cottage which was occupied by John Boulter and his wife Sally. Just beyond the archway and alongside us was the door to cottage no. 5 that housed Mike Williams and his wife Gill.

John taught French, I think. He was an athlete of distinction yet quietly unassuming about his successes, representing Britain internationally on the track in the 800 metres and the mile. Mike taught craft and design – he refused to be called the woodwork master. He was an ebullient Welshman and a man of action. Mike had a brown belt in judo. He also had an air rifle which he used on pigeons invading his allotment. The birds may well have ended their days as a roast on his dinner table along with the fruit and vegetables he grew in the Thirlestaine Cottages gardens. John, Sally, Mike and Gill were good friends as well as close neighbours.

Although I remember nothing of that first term of teaching at the College, two incidents have stuck in my mind. One occurred before term began. The other occurred in the Christmas holiday.

That doggie in the courtyard

We had just about moved into 4 Thirlestaine Cottage when our two-year old daughter, Alison, saw a large dog running across the end of the courtyard. She called out to me and pointed at it. 'That's a Dalmatian, Alison,' I said.

Later that day the four of us were invited to the home of Hugh Wright, one of the teachers and a senior tutor (called the Driver) at Cheltondale House - the boarding house of my tutees. Hugh ushered us into the lounge and offered us tea and cake. We had barely settled into our seats, when the door opened and Hugh's wife came in. With her was the large dog we had seen running across our courtyard.

The dog bounded around licking everybody in sight. Our 4-month old son, Stephen, was out of reach clinging to my wife, Maureen. Alison and I were fair game for Sam – I think that was the dog's name. Hugh's wife smiled at our daughter and said, 'Sam won't bite you. He's a nice doggie.' Alison, our two-year old, looked up and said, 'Sam's a lovely Dalmatian, isn't he?'

The Mad Axeman

Cheltenham Spa sits in a valley on the edge of the Cotswolds hills. It has been a holiday and health resort since the discovery of the mineral springs in 1716. The inhabitants are by and large respectable and affluent. The town is famous for its Regency architecture and its steeplechase horseracing. It tends to be a relatively sleepy place, especially in the warm, humid summertime. Cheltenham College (locally known as the gentlemen's college) and Cheltenham Ladies College provide an excellent boarding school education for the sons and daughters of any parents but especially of military men and statesmen often on the move. The town motto is *Salubritas et Erudito* (Health and Education). Cheltenham is a safe place to live as a rule.

Just before term ended, the newspapers, television and radio were full of the escape from Dartmoor of Frank Mitchell. In the cloistered world of the College, pupils and teachers alike were too busy to pay much attention to the news reports. Our principal concern was the end of term reports. The only escape of interest was of pupils from the demands of their teachers and vice versa. Even when term finally ended and, in the words our Head of History and Cadet Corps Commander, all was quiet on the Western Front, nobody gave thought to Frank Mitchell. Over the end of term drinks in the common room, the topic did come up in the conversation.

'The poor beggar's probably on foot,' said a geographer. 'He'll have his work cut out getting to Cheltenham. Devon and Gloucestershire counties are over 100 miles apart. Mind you, if he ran as fast as Boulter's last mile, he could be here in a day.'

'Nobody ever escapes from *the moor*,' said a young physics master in an eerie voice.

'You've been reading too many of those Agatha Christie *penny dreadfuls*,' snorted the Head of English. 'At least the Times correctly stated this fellow Mitchell absconded from the prison. He did not escape. He just walked off.'

'Why is he called The Mad Axeman?' asked another colleague.

'According to the Times,' said our Head of English, 'he was in and out of institutions from the age of seventeen. He escaped from Broadmoor, broke into an elderly couple's home and held them hostage. According to one report he made them drink tea and watch television with him while he balanced across his knees an axe he'd found in their garden shed. He never actually harmed them. Mr Frank Mitchell is said to have the mind of a child and to be given to tantrums.'

'So, he's harmless then?' said the young physicist.

'I think not,' said our Times reader. 'It seems he is a giant of a man and as strong as an ox. Certainly *not* an opponent for the holder of a mere brown belt,' he said looking at Mike Williams.

Christmas was soon upon us. We were just about ready for my parents when they arrived on Christmas Eve. They had driven from Bristol, our home town, and brought their overnight things and presents for their grandchildren. Christmas Day came and went in a blur of opening presents, overeating at lunchtime (turkey with all the trimmings followed by traditional pudding and brandy sauce) and washing up the dishes, pots and pans.

After the struggle to keep awake in front of the TV during the Queen's 3 o'clock speech to the Commonwealth, we woke up to assemble and play with various toys before overeating at teatime (sandwiches, trifle with real whipped cream followed by a slice of iced Christmas cake – no Alison, the snowman on the top is not edible). After more washing up and putting the children to bed, we collapsed in front of the TV. There were warnings about Frank Mitchell.

'The mad axeman is still at large. According to the police, Frank Mitchell is not armed but he is dangerous. Members of the public are advised not to approach him. Unconfirmed reports say that he was last seen in the Gloucester area.'

I switched off the television. We were all ready for bed. Alison and Stephen were already asleep in their room. My parents went to sleep in our bedroom over the archway. Maureen and I had our convertible bed-settee in the lounge. That night everybody slept soundly and safely in their beds.

The sound of the electric milk float at the end of the driveway and the clink of milk bottles woke me up at about 6 a.m. I slid out of the bed-settee, put on my dressing gown and made my way to the front door to catch the milkman. I pulled back the catch and peeped out.

'Merry Christmas,' I said, handing the milkman a few shillings.

'Thank you, Sir. Merry Christmas to you too.'

'Bit chilly this morning?'

'It is that,' he said, 'but at least it's dry. Not going away?'

'No. Can't afford it.'

'Have Mr and Mrs Boulter gone away?'

'Yes, I'm sure they have. Why do you ask?'

'Their front door's ajar.'

'Really? That's not like them. They wouldn't leave their place unlocked. I'll take a look.'

Sure enough it was ajar - only slightly – but nevertheless it was unlocked and open.

I retreated into our cottage to consider what I should do. *Unconfirmed reports said the mad axeman was last seen in the*

Gloucester area. Thirlestaine Cottages were accessible from the main road and also through the gardens. What if Frank Mitchell was inside no. 6 cottage? What if he wasn't and instead the Boulters had let friends of Mike and Gill use it while they were away? If I woke up Mike at 6 o'clock on Boxing morning (how apt a name) and his friends were in the Boulters' cottage, he would not be pleased, to put it mildly. If his friends were not using no. 6 and Mike thought Frank Mitchell was inside, he might be daft enough to don his judo kit and brown belt to try a citizen's arrest. I decided to play safe. I dialled 999.

'Which emergency service do you require? Ambulance, police or fire brigade?'

'Police, please.'

'Just one moment.'

'Police!'

It took me just a couple of minutes to give the desk sergeant my name and address, to explain why I was calling and to apologise in case I might be doing the wrong thing. Within less than five minutes of my making that call, an unmarked car came quietly to a halt at the end of the driveway and courtyard. Still in my pyjamas, dressing gown and slippers, I went outside in time to see four very large uniformed policemen getting out of the car. One was an officer, one was a sergeant and the other two were constables. I spoke to the officer in charge.

'The Boulters are away. Their door is open but doesn't look to have been forced. I've probably dragged you out on a wild goose chase.'

'You did the right thing, Sir. I just wish more people would be as alert and co-operative. Would you lead the way, please.'

I lead the way to no. 6 and showed them the open front door.

'Just stand back, Sir, if you please,' said the officer. 'Right, lads, quietly now.'

The four policemen stepped into the hallway, not noisily but not particularly quietly either. They entered two-by-two. The first two were the tallest – more than 6ft 6in plus helmet. The other two were not much shorter. I followed behind at 5ft 8in in my slippers. The door straight ahead led into the lounge. A constable pushed it open and switched on the light. The officer turned and asked me to take a look inside. I did. It was a shambles. All sorts of stuff, mostly clothing, was strewn everywhere.

'Mr and Mrs Boulter tidy people, Sir?' asked the officer in a whisper.

'Yes, they are,' I whispered back,' as the constable switched off the light.

'Right, lads! Let's have a look upstairs,' said the officer switching on the light at the top of the stairs.

Two-by-two, the tallest in the front, they walked, not crept, up the stairs. I followed in darkness – they were so tall that they blotted out the light. The five of us gathered on the landing outside the first bedroom. The door was ajar. We listened. We could hear breathing from within. In a normal voice, the officer instructed the tallest constable to take a look inside without turning on the light. He did.

'There's a baby asleep in here,' he reported to the officer. My heart sank. The Boulters didn't have any children. I was asked to take a look.

'I'm sorry. I have never seen this baby before,' I whispered when the constable shone his torch on the cot. We came out of the bedroom and moved along to the next door.

'In you go, lad,' said the officer to the constable. In he went. And in we all went. The constable shone his torch onto the couple seemingly sound asleep. Then we all stepped out onto the landing and the constable closed the bedroom door.

'That was definitely not Mr and Mrs Boulter,' I said. 'My guess is they're friends of my neighbours in no. 5 cottage. I really am sorry to have dragged you here on a fool's errand.'

'All in a day's work, Sir. You've nothing to be sorry about. You did the right thing.'

That was not what Mike Williams said to me later that morning!

* * * * *

Epilogue

The people in the cottage were friends of Mike and Gill Williams. The policemen never woke up the baby but, as I learned later, they did wake up the parents who were so terrified that they kept their eyes tight shut throughout, fearing the worst was about to happen to them.

Mike was unconvinced by my logic for calling the police and never saw any reason for telling us his friends would be staying in no. 6. Neither did he seemed concerned that his friends had not locked up properly. My parents in our bedroom over the archway and our children slept soundly through it all.

It appears that the Kray Twins (Ronnie and Reggie - Britain's notorious London East End gangsters in the 1950s and 1960s, who befriended Frank Mitchell when they were in Wandsworth prison together) masterminded his getaway from Dartmoor. They kept him hidden in London. By the 23rd of December 1966 Frank Mitchell was probably dead, shot by one the gang.

Cheltenham College is now co-educational. Thirlestaine House and the Cottages are listed buildings of historic interest. Thirlestaine Cottages have now become part of Westal House where the girls are boarded.

* * * * *

A Tick in a Box

A Canadian source defines bureaucracy as a hierarchy of authority and a system of rules, regulations and record keeping characterized by division of labour and specialization of functions. A British source defines bureaucracy as an excessively complicated administrative procedure. After reading this story, the reader will, I trust, take more care than I did when completing any official form but heed the words of Robert Frost, "If we couldn't laugh, we would all go insane."

* * * * *

Let me state unequivocally that I have never suffered from hypochondriasis. I have never been a hypochondriac. I do not have a chronic abnormal anxiety about the state of my health. Quite to the contrary, symptoms and evidence of illness or disease revealed by a medical examination do not make me anxious - they intrigue me. My wife has commented, more than once I think, that I should probably find my own death intriguing. Perhaps I shall. I am, however, in no hurry to experience that once-in-a-lifetime, not-to-be-repeated event.

In the summer of 1961, I damaged my right knee playing cricket. In the summer of 1976, I had the two wisdom teeth extracted from my lower jaw. In the late autumn of 1976, I started to see (against cloudless skies and plain white walls) numerous dark threads and spots swirling before my eyes. Then one Monday my right knee and my lower jaw started to hurt. It was time to consult my doctor. I telephoned the surgery. 'Brrrring, brrrring, brrrring.'

'Hadleigh House! Just one moment. Beep... Beep... Beep... Beep...' almost ad infinitum. 'Sorry to keep you waiting. Can I have your name please?'

'I'd like to see Dr. Fleming, please.'

'Are you a patient of Dr Fleming?'

'Yes!'

'Can I have your name please?

I gave my surname and then, as demanded, my Christian name.

'What's wrong with you, Michael?'

'That's what I expect Dr Fleming to find out.'

'Is it an emergency?'

'Is Dr Fleming in this afternoon?'

'No. He's on holiday. I can fit you in at 4:30 to see his locum, Dr Benjamin.'

'Thank you. I'll be at the Hadleigh House surgery at 4:30.'

At 4:25 I reported to the receptionist and would-be diagnostician in the white coat behind the desk of the appointments office. She ticked me off – that is my name on a list not me personally – and waved me toward a seat in the waiting area. I turned a blind eye to the ancient, well-thumbed magazines and a deaf ear to the background music accompanying the coughing and sneezing of my waiting companions. My attention was drawn to the pamphlets and posters urging me to take more exercise, eat less salt, butter, etc. and telling me what to do in the event of a heart attack or a stroke. My name was called before I could tackle the leaflet on cancer.

'What seems to be the trouble?'

I started at the top and worked my way downwards. First, the spots before my eyes.

'Those spots and threads are floaters. They're caused by dead cells or tiny spots of blood leaking into the vitreous fluid. They're quite common and nothing to worry about,' he said putting the ophthalmoscope back in its case.

'I had my wisdom teeth removed about two months ago at Poole Hospital,' I said in response to his question. 'Ever since then my jaw makes a knocking sound when I chew or yawn. It only became painful this past weekend.'

'Rest your jaw as much as possible and if you must yawn, try to keep your mouth closed. Make an appointment to see Dr Fleming if the pain gets any worse.'

'I damaged my knee playing cricket fifteen years ago. Every now and then, it swells up and the joint becomes painful. It's quite random.'

'Did they operate on your knee when you first went to the hospital after the match?'

'They aspirated two and one-half ounces of blood and fluid. Otherwise, no.'

'You've probably damaged the cartilage. Arthritis may be setting in. If the swelling and pain start to occur more often and more regularly, Dr Fleming will probably arrange for an X-ray. Anything else?'

'No, thank you, that's it for now.'

* * * * *

The following Monday morning I arrived early at school. My instructions had arrived from the Examination Board. In the office I lifted the heavy electric typewriter from the desk where I wanted to work and put it on the floor by the desk. When the bell rang for the start of morning school, I picked up the typewriter to put it back on the desk and felt a momentary twinge in my groin.

When I returned to our newly built house that afternoon, there waiting for me on the front porch were the ten laminated boards (each 8 ft x 2 ft and rather heavy) I had ordered. They would become built-in wardrobes in our new house. I carried each board separately to my workshop at the back of the garage. When I had deposited the last one, I put my hand in my trouser pocket for my handkerchief and felt a large lump in my groin. I consulted my Reader's Digest Family Medical Adviser.

Hernia – protrusion of abdominal organs through a gap in the abdominal wall. Inguinal hernia is the most common type of rupture in males. The bulge can be very large – up to 6 inches – and occurs in the groin crease.

Under the subheading *When to consult a doctor* I read that strangulation may occur and cut off the blood supply to the bowel and cause gangrene. I picked up the telephone and rang the Hadleigh House surgery.

'Dr Fleming is still on holiday. Is it an emergency?'

'Not yet but it soon could be.'

'Dr Benjamin has had a cancellation. I can fit you in at 5 o'clock.'

I reported to the receptionist behind the appointments desk and looked for that pamphlet on cancer. Just as I reached the section on birthmarks and the risk of skin cancer, my name was called.

'Michael. Room 3.'

I knocked on the door and entered.

'Lie down on the couch please.' The locum, Dr Benjamin, was sitting at a desk in the far corner with his back to the door and the couch. I did as I was told.

'Have your ankles and feet been swelling in the evenings?'

'No.'

'Any loss of breath going upstairs?'

'No.'

'What about a cough? Have you been coughing a lot recently?'

'No.'

'Have you stopped smoking?'

'Yes. No. Sorry. I never started. I'm a non-smoker. I always have been.'

'What about alcohol? Would you say you're a heavy drinker?'

'No. I might have a small glass of sherry occasionally. I don't drink beer. If we have friends in, I usually join them in a glass of wine with our meal.'

After a few more questions which seemed to me to have nothing at all to do with hernias, I blurted out, 'Excuse me! Who do you think you're talking to?' He turned to look at me lying there on the couch. I realised that I had sounded like a schoolmaster dressing down a pupil who'd had the nerve to answer me back. I rephrased the question and used a more polite tone of voice. 'Who do you think I am?'

That still didn't sound quite right, so I tried, 'What do you think my name is?' When he said Leonard Watson, I said, 'No. Mr Watson cancelled his appointment. I'm the patient you saw last Monday. You know, spots before the eyes; knocking sounds in the jaw; a swollen right knee. As a slightly strange look came over his face, I said reassuringly, 'I think I've got a hernia this week!'

* * * * *

My wife drove me to the local cottage hospital. I took with me my pyjamas, my tooth brush and paste, my electric razor and the thirty chemistry notebooks I had to mark. I signed in, changed into my pyjamas and sat on the bed to mark the books. Matron arrived in full sail.

With a firm hand and an air of unquestioned and unquestionable authority, she placed a form on the book I was marking and ordered me to fill it in immediately. I did so as quickly as possible because I wanted to finish my marking before evening visiting hour. My wife promised to return the books to my school the next day and allow me to relax for the next six or seven weeks.

The form was small (A5 = 148 mm wide and 210 mm long). The spaces on the front for me to write my name, address, etc., were very small. On the back of the form there was a question which simply required a tick in the appropriate box.

| Was your injury the result of an industrial accident?   Yes ☐   No ☐ |

'Well,' I thought to myself, 'I was at work and I ruptured myself by picking up that heavy electric typewriter that belonged to the school.' I put a tick in the 'Yes box' and returned to my marking. That evening my wife took the chemistry notebooks away and I lay back on my bed to await the anaesthetist. When he knew I was a chemist, he was pleased to give me the details of the pre-op injection (to make me drowsy) and the anaesthetic gas (to keep me asleep). That night I slept as soundly as I always do but this time on an empty stomach.

The next morning I was wheeled into the antechamber. I remember counting down from 100 to 96. And then, there I was back in my bed in the ward slowly waking up to the voice of the staff nurse calling my name.

That afternoon my wife came to see me. I was so hungry that I persuaded the nurse to let me have some jelly and ice cream. It was a mistake. The picture in my wife's mind - of me losing that dessert - was not one she would want to paint for our two young children.

Early that evening, after visiting hour, I fell into my usual deep, restful sleep. At about ten o'clock, a disembodied voice was calling me. At first it was part of my dream. It was unreal. The voice kept calling my name. Gradually the dream faded and my mind slowly and reluctantly entered into the real world. The night nurse was standing by my bed.

'What is it?' I mumbled. 'What's wrong? What do you want?'

'Sit up,' she said, handing me a glass of water and a small plastic cup holding a huge white tablet.

'What's this?' I asked.

'Come along now. No fuss. There's a good chap,' she said sternly. 'Take your tablet.'

Then it began to dawn on me. 'Is this nitrazepam?' I asked.

'It's Mogadon,' she replied.

'I was sound asleep! You woke me up to give me enough nitrazepam to knock out a cart horse!'

'Matron's orders and hospital rules. You had an operation today so we need to make sure you get a good night's sleep.'

'But I was getting a good night's sleep until you woke me up!' I mumbled as she moved to the sleeping victim in the next bed. The Mogadon (trade name for nitrazepam) soon did its job. It put me to sleep and ensured that the next morning I woke with a blinding headache to go with the pain in my groin.

The breakfast trolley appeared. The food and the aspirins were just what I needed. What I didn't need after breakfast was Matron in full sail. 'Everybody up and into the lounge.' When I said that I was very sore from my operation yesterday and would prefer to stay in bed, she snorted, 'No excuses and no exceptions. This ward has to be cleaned.'

It was only when I started to plan how I might get out of bed with the minimum of pain that I noticed how far off the ground I was. A step ladder hooked to the bed frame would not have been out of place. Those old-fashioned static beds kept the patient so high off the ground that I wouldn't have been surprised if the nurses had to satisfy a minimum height requirement similar to that of police officers.

The meals in the hospital were delicious, nutritious and nicely balanced. When I left there nine days after my operation, I was a good deal slimmer than when I had entered. I had been treated well but there was no place like home especially to enjoy seven weeks convalescence on full pay and on doctor's orders not to lift even a dish cloth.

* * * * *

About a year later I was back in the hospital for repair and maintenance. Curiously enough, I had very little post-operative pain this second time. Moreover, the surgeon had followed the line of his original incision, so I actually have only one scar to show for two operations. I was incarcerated for nine days again and subject to the same Matron but in a different ward.

The food was still nourishing and the beds still frighteningly high off the ground. The nurse administered as before a Mogadon on the night of the operation. Just before I fell asleep, I was aware of noises emanating from an elderly patient. He seemed to be groaning and moaning in dire pain. His bed was nearest to the night nurse's observation window. My bed was the furthest away. Incidentally, I later learned that the nearer you were to the nurse's window the more serious was your condition.

On the first night, the patients in nearby beds were kept awake for hours by what they thought was his snoring. With each successive night, his groaning, moaning and, perhaps, snoring became more structured. A pattern developed. The noises began to rise and fall and sound like notes. It was on the eighth night that his racket began to sound like words being sung to a tune. On my last night the form, pattern and shape of his sounds became clear. The old fellow was not groaning, moaning or snoring. He was singing, albeit not very tunefully and perhaps in his sleep, the old hymn Oh God our help in ages past!

* * * * *

Several months after the second operation I received a letter from an official in the Department of Health and Social Security (DHSS) requesting my presence at the Council Building in the Civic Centre in Poole. I presented myself as requested and was led into a tiny room. The official was a pleasant lady, probably in her mid-forties (but I'm a poor judge of women's ages) and, as I recall, unmarried. We sat opposite each other on either side of a small table. The interview began.

'Full name?' An easy question to start.

'Date of birth? Present address? Occupation?' More straightforward questions.

'May I ask what this is all about?' I said politely.

'Your claim for compensation.'

'I'm sorry,' I said, 'I don't understand. What claim?'

'For the injury you sustained as the result of an industrial accident. May we continue?'

Then I remembered.

Was your injury the result of an industrial accident?	Yes ☑	No ☐

I ticked the Yes box on the back of that form Matron gave me.

'Where did you get the injury?'

'In the school office when I picked up a heavy typewriter.'

'No, sorry. Where did you sustain the injury?'

'As I just said, in the office at the school where I teach.'

'No,' she said, beginning to blush, 'where on your body did you sustain the injury?'

'It was an inguinal hernia. Would you like to see?' I asked, starting to get up and reach for the buckle of the belt holding up my trousers.

'Thank you. No, thank you. That will not be necessary,' she said, her face crimson as she hurried from the room.

* * * * *

A year must have passed before I received further instructions from the DHSS to attend another interview. This time I was summoned to a set of offices in Bournemouth. I taught my first class before driving the 9 miles into the seaside town. When I climbed the stairs and entered the large reception room, I was summoned to the desk of a rather frosty-faced young lady.

I handed her the official letter I had received. With barely a glance at me standing there, she began her questions. Name? Date of Birth? Address? Occupation? The self same questions I had already answered in the Poole Office. Fortunately, this young lady seemed to know the nature of my industrial injury and did not inquire as to its location on my body.

'Follow me.'

I followed her across the room.

'Take off your shoes and stand against the wall.'

'Why?'

'I have to measure your height.'

I did as I was told but received no reply when I asked why she needed my height.

'Stand on the scales.'

'Why?'

'I have to measure your weight.'

I didn't expect an explanation so I didn't bother to ask why.

'Put on your shoes and take a seat.'

It was nice to be able to sit down at last. Some time later, Ms Frosty, ushered me into another equally large room where I was confronted by three elderly, grey-haired men sitting behind a large cloth-covered table. The old fellow in the middle directed me to sit in the chair facing them. This chairman carefully shuffled some papers before beginning the interview.

Name? Date of Birth? Address? Occupation? All the questions I had already answered in the outer office. During this questioning I could have sworn one of his cohorts was dozing off. The other one never spoke either. And he didn't move. Had I been able to get a closer look – my chair was a considerable distance from their table – I might have seen cobwebs joining his head to the table top.

I wondered if they were medical doctors and if they would ask to see my injury. They were but they didn't ask. It was just as well. The wound had had a year to heal. The scar was barely visible. I assumed they constituted a panel to investigate the validity of compensation claims for industrial injuries. If so, I am bound to wonder if they ever exposed any frauds.

I returned to the outer office and Miss Frosty.

'Where have you come from?'

'The inner sanctum,' I said flippantly. She was not amused.

'Where did you come from to get here this morning?'

When I told her the name of the school where I was teaching, she thawed.

'Is that the grammar school?'

When I said yes, she beamed at me. 'Do you know Martin Sandel?'

'Yes, I know Boot,' I said, referring to his nickname. 'Do you know him?'

She blushed. 'Did you come by car?

'Yes.'

'How far is the round trip from the grammar school to here and back again?'

'About 18 miles.'

She multiplied 18 by 35 and gave me £6.30 travelling expenses.

Several weeks later I received an official letter from the DHSS stating that my claim had been approved. Enclosed with the letter was a £15.75 cheque and a receipt for me to sign and return to confirm that I was satisfied and accepted the payment in full and final settlement of my claim. My scar reminds me to think twice before putting a tick in Yes boxes on official forms.

* * * * *

Epilogue

My two nine-day spells in that cottage hospital were luxuries not available to hernia patients these days. Now you are usually treated as an outpatient to be cut open, stitched up before lunch and sent home in the afternoon. Of course, that may not be the case if you can afford to be treated as a private patient! As for convalescence, four weeks seems to be regarded as more than generous.

The bureaucratic machine in which I became entangled and the bureaucratic cogs whom I encountered made me ill-tempered and, on reflection, unforgivably flippant. Given the chance, I should like to apologise to those officials who were probably doing what they could to follow the rules and make the best of a poor job.

Even though those entanglements were almost 40 years in my distant past, I still have difficulty taking comfort from the words of the Pulitzer Prize-winning American poet, Robert Frost, "If we couldn't laugh, we would all go insane."

THE JOURNEY OF A CANVAS BAG

Air is a liquid at minus 200 degrees centigrade. In their research at Bristol University, chemistry students often needed liquid air for their experiments. They kept the liquid in open-necked vacuum flasks to slow its evaporation. This story is based upon an incident that actually took place on a train travelling from Bristol to Southampton around 1958-59. Apart from Bob, all the characters are figments of my imagination. Two of the characters appear in the first story in volume 2 of my collected short stories.

* * * * *

On any other Friday Bob would have slung his canvas bag of weekend clothes over his shoulder, run down University Road, jumped onto the bus to Temple Meads Station and taken a seat upstairs. Not this Friday. Today Bob held his bag upright against his chest. He walked slowly down the hill. He boarded the double-decker bus as smoothly as possible and did not go upstairs. He took the seat downstairs nearest the door. Getting off the bus and walking to the station platform, he was just as careful not to bump into people or to jolt his bag. He only started to relax after he gently placed his bag upright on the small table under the window of the 2nd class non-smoking compartment.

Before taking his window seat facing the engine, Bob cautiously unzipped his almost empty bag to check the contents and to remove a hardback edition of Organic Chemistry by Fieser & Fieser. As he carefully closed the zip he smiled nervously at the grey-haired lady in the window seat opposite. She returned his smile then quickly looked back at her knitting pattern. Bob sat down and hid behind his bag and textbook.

Daphne Millbank SRN smiled politely but did not speak. 'Quite handsome,' she thought, 'but a rather nervous young man,' His textbook and the badge on his dark blazer showed he was a chemistry student at Bristol University. She remembered the engineering undergraduate she danced with at her Nursing College Christmas Hop some thirty years ago. He had the same good looks - dark hair and soulful brown eyes.

Under other circumstances Daphne might have spoken to Bob if he had not disappeared behind his textbook and that large canvas bag. Anyway, she had a problem to solve and travellers in England keep themselves to themselves. Before Daphne could focus her thoughts, a smartly-dressed, slightly balding, puffy-faced man with a touch of grey at his temples made his entrance. She smiled. He frowned. She refocused on her problem.

* * * * *

Aubrey Pembleton-Smythe squinted into the sunshine as he left the gloomy offices of Hudson Smith, Briggs & Co. in Unity Street. He used this prestigious firm of chartered accounts to audit his accounts principally to impress the more wealthy of his clients whose investments he managed. The meeting had gone well. The senior accountants seemed satisfied with his explanations of certain entries in his books - the set of books he kept especially for them. Their final audited statements would, hopefully, satisfy the Inland Revenue. From the waistcoat pocket of his dark grey, pin-striped suit Aubrey took a silver watch and opened its case. Half-past one already! Too late for a bus! So he walked briskly the short distance to Park Street and hailed a taxi.

At Temple Meads Station Sid, a seasoned porter, materialised from the archway shadows and opened the taxi door. Aubrey handed him his dark imitation leather brief case, paid the taxi driver the exact amount on the meter and waved the porter towards the platform for the 2:15 train to Southampton. 'Smart three-piece, shiny leather shoes, lightweight briefcase, no luggage - First Class and nice tip down to expenses,' thought Sid. But when Aubrey specified a second-class compartment and non-smoking, Sid gave up any thoughts of a gratuity. Sure enough, at the door of the compartment, Sid was relieved of the briefcase and, like the taxi driver, dismissed without a word of thanks.

Aubrey frowned. Both seats by the window were occupied. And there was a large bag filling the little table where he would have put his briefcase, lid open, to hide from the gaze of that old biddy. 'Little privacy on this journey,' he thought. In his case was, as usual, his expenses notebook. But today he also had the first of two volumes by Count Egon Caesar Corti - The Rise of the House of Rothschild: 1770-1830. The second volume - The Reign of the House of Rothschild: 1830-1871 was locked away on his bookshelf in Southampton. These rare first editions, published in 1928, were English translations by Brian and Beatrix Lunn from German. First, his day's expenses. He preferred to record them while the train was stationary.

Aubrey sat by the door in the corner seat facing the engine. Resting his notebook on his briefcase he calligraphically recorded the published cost of a breakfast on the train, a lunch at the station, taxi fares including tips and a First Class Southampton-Bristol return rail fare. That done, he put away the expenses notebook, took out volume 1 and placed the case on the seat opposite. He had just opened his book when a slender young woman entered the compartment. He studied her over the top of his half-moon reading glasses.

* * * * *

Her straight fair hair was held back by two brown tortoiseshell clips. Her eyes were green behind a pair of rimless spectacles. Her skin seemed pale against her tailored dark olive jacket and skirt. The dark brown of her sensible flat-heeled shoes almost matched the colour of her real leather briefcase – a 21st birthday gift four years ago from her parents. She glanced at his imitation leather briefcase then sat down next to the grey-haired lady.

That morning, Miss Rachel Wallace, B.Econ., had visited Hudson Smith, Briggs & Co. on behalf of the Inland Revenue Investigation Office. Mr. de Veen, one of the senior accountants, had been most helpful in giving her access to their records and a quiet room where she would not be disturbed. It had been a most fruitful visit.

Stepping into the compartment she noticed the embossed letters A.P-S before she saw the owner of the case. She recognised Aubrey immediately from the flattering photograph in the file, marked *Confidential/Investigate*, given to her three days ago by her Head of Department. 'Looks younger in his photograph,' she mused, noticing his sallow podgy face, receding hairline and advancing waistline.

She put her briefcase on the luggage rack above her head and sat a short distance from the grey-haired lady. They exchanged smiles. 'A nurse,' she thought when she saw the upside-down watch pinned on Daphne's crisp white blouse. Rachel folded The Daily Telegraph, took out a pencil and started the cryptic crossword on the back page.

1. across – reduce payment this way and go directly to gaol – 3,7.

She smiled to herself as she filled in the letters. Rachel was still smiling to herself when she glanced up at the tall man standing in the doorway. His face seemed familiar.

84

Johannes van Dijk looked every inch a Dutchman – six feet tall with blond hair, blue eyes, high round cheekbones, a wide mouth and even white teeth smiling back at Rachel. Under his brown suede leather jacket and silk shirt were a pair of broad shoulders and muscular arms. 'Good afternoon everyone,' he said in a clear voice. When Aubrey glanced up from his book, Johannes, still smiling, said to him, 'Allow me to put your briefcase up here, please,' And in an instant Aubrey found his case on the luggage rack above his head.

One moment later Johannes had effortlessly hoisted his own heavy portmanteau (real cowhide leather and solid brass buckles) onto the rack on his own side and seated himself by the door opposite Aubrey. The ensuing silence was broken by the sound of doors slamming and the guard's whistle. With a slight jolt the 14:15 Southampton train started to move.

'3 minutes late,' muttered Aubrey looking at his pocket watch.

'The train is late or perhaps your watch is not good,' said Johannes.

'This watch keeps excellent time,' snapped Aubrey, 'This train is always late.'

'Not so in Holland. Our trains are never late.'

Daphne looked down at her watch and said to Rachel, ''Yes, the train does seem to be 3 minutes late.'

'What's three minutes,' said Rachel. 'The engine driver could easily catch up the time lost.'

'Most unlikely,' snorted Aubrey, as he closed his pocket watch.

'That seems a very fine watch,' said Johannes. 'May I look at it closely?'

Before Aubrey could reply, Johannes took hold of the watch. He knew it. It was a rare Paul Buhre antique - a Swiss full hunter style pocket watch. The case, almost certainly made of solid 925 Sterling silver, was about 51 mm thick and had solid rose gold hinges. Johannes opened the front cover. The ceramic dial behind the gold hands was in perfect condition. There was an inscription on the inside of the case:

Pieter van Dijk
Middleburg – 1881 tot 1911
in dankbaarheid voor uwe trouwe dienst

He frowned and said softly, 'Ongelofelijk! Hoe kan dat?'

'I beg your pardon,' said Aubrey.

'Sorry. Unbelievable! How could it be… No, I mean… is it possible you would sell to me this watch? I should very much like to have it.'

Aubrey Pembleton-Smythe was taken aback. He closed his eyes in thought. He had redeemed the watch a few years ago from a pawnbroker. A passenger getting off at Warminster had dropped the pawn ticket getting up to leave the train - this one in fact - the 14:15 Bristol to Southampton. It cost Aubrey just £17.50. He now regarded the timepiece as an heirloom of the Pembleton-Smythe family. Pure fantasy, of course, just like his name. He had been born Arthur Smith but changed his name by deed-poll to Aubrey Pembleton-Smythe to boost his self-esteem before going to college to study accounting and economics.

'This watch has been in my family a long time,' lied Aubrey smoothly. 'It's not something an Englishman would think to part with easily.'

'Yes, I understand that. No offence, you know. But, I should very much like to have that watch. I can pay cash. What cost would you consider fair?'

Aubrey took back the watch and closed his eyes again. Bob appeared engrossed in his Organic textbook but Daphne and Rachel were fascinated. Johannes smiled broadly and winked at them. 'Well? What say you? Will you sell me the watch? I can give you cash now.' Johannes took out and opened his genuine leather wallet. Aubrey lifted his lids and his eyes bulged at the sight of so many £10 notes. He opened his mouth to speak just as the compartment door slid open. 'Tickets please,' demanded the guard.

* * * * *

Daphne and Rachel quickly located their tickets which the guard carefully checked and punched. The guard nodded at Bob's student pass. A somewhat flustered Aubrey eventually produced his ticket from behind the maroon silk handkerchief in his top pocket. He handed it over. The guard checked the ticket very carefully, punched it, checked again even more carefully then handed it back. Aubrey frowned but said nothing. Johannes took a ticket out of his bulging wallet. 'Please,' he said with a smile to the guard.

'When and where did you buy this ticket, sir?' asked the guard.

'I did not myself buy it. It was my secretary. She is responsible. Is it not good?'

'Oh, no, sir. The ticket is valid for this journey but…'

'But what?' frowned Johannes.

'It's for First Class, sir. You are in the wrong compartment.'

'Ah. This is because I followed this gentleman who I should think to go First Class.'

'The First Class compartment is two carriages that way,' said the guard pointing down the corridor. 'It's next to the dining car.'

'Thank you,' said Johannes, 'but I stay here. It is gezellig – cosy.'

'It's up to you,' said the guard. 'Next stop Bath Spa.'

When the door had closed, the Dutchman turned and noticed Aubrey's book – green cloth with black labels and decorated endpapers.

'What is the book you read?'

Aubrey showed him the cover.

'A rare first edition,' thought Johannes. 'Does he realise?' Then he said, 'Do you also have volume 2?'

'At home under lock and key,' replied Aubrey.

'Ah, so. Now, you will sell me that watch, yes? I have money – cash.'

These conversations had distracted Daphne. As she put her ticket back into her purse she remembered her problem. She had been invited to stay with Frank and Susan, her niece, in Bitterne for a few days. Susan was expecting her first baby any time now. On this two-hour journey to Southampton Daphne wanted to knit a pair of booties for the baby. The problem was what colour? What if she knitted a blue pair and Susan had a girl? The lady sitting next to her seemed very sensible. They had already smiled and spoken to one another. Perhaps she would help?

'Easy,' said Rachel. 'Knit one pair of each colour.'

'I'm quite a good knitter,' said Daphne, 'but I'm not sure I could knit two pairs before we reach Southampton.'

'Well then,' said Rachel, 'knit one of each colour now, When you know what it is - boy or girl - you can knit the other bootie before you visit your niece in the maternity ward. Perhaps she'll have twins – boy and girl. You'd have a pair of booties for each baby in no time.'

Bob listened to this conversation behind his textbook and wondered if he had solved his problem. Only time would tell. At least the guard had not asked him to put his hold-all on the luggage rack. And so far he'd managed to keep it upright and not to jolt it. It was tempting to check inside the bag again but he decided to leave well alone.

'What colour booties? Some problem,' thought Rachel. 'I wish my investigation could be solved so easily. I've seen the set of books he gave to Hudson Smith, Briggs & Co. He'll have his other set pretty well hidden. The guard seemed wary of him. Took his time checking the ticket. Still, he didn't query it. So he's definitely travelling on a valid Second Class ticket and not First Class as this other passenger thought. When I get to his office on Monday I'll ask for his expenses notebooks and all his actual receipts for the last six years. That should shake things up a bit.' With a smile she turned her attention to a tall blond fellow sitting nearby. His face did seem familiar.

When the train stopped, Johannes asked Rachel, 'What is this place?'

'Bath,' said Rachel. 'Bath Spa, actually. It's a cathedral city. The Roman Baths were built around the only naturally occurring hot springs in Britain.'

'This I did not know,' said Johannes.

'Apparently,' continued Rachel, looking at Aubrey out of the corner of her eye, 'in Roman times, if thieves stole a bather's money or clothes, the bather would write on a piece of metal – called a curse tablet - to the goddess Sulis Minerva asking her to punish the thieves until they gave the money and clothes back.'

'You like Bath Spa?'

'Yes, very much,' said Rachel.

'Perhaps I shall make a visit there.'

'Oh you should,' said Rachel enthusiastically. 'There is so much to see and learn.'

'When I shall go there you must come with me as my personal guide. Is that possible?'

Rachel blushed and said as the train moved off, 'Westbury is our next stop.'

'Should I make also a visit there?' asked Johannes.

'It's not at all like Bath. There's nothing to see except the Westbury White Horse. Scholars say it was cut into the chalk hillside sometime in the late eighteenth century. Locals claim the horse appeared more than eleven hundred years ago to commemorate King Alfred the Great's victory over the Danes.'

* * * * *

It suddenly occurred to Aubrey that he did not know the true value of the watch. How could he estimate it. Ah! Assume the pawnbroker knew his business. Assume the £17.50 redemption cost included a £2.50 interest charge on a loan of £15. Assume the pawnbroker lends only 10% of the value of the article pawned. That would make the watch worth about £150. Perhaps more if the £150 represents the pawnbroker's resale value – say, 60% of the actual value. He looked at the Dutchman and said, 'I cannot put a value on this watch. Perhaps you would tell me how much you would be willing to pay.'

'That's not so easy,' said Johannes. 'One should be an expert and I do not want to insult you. Furthermore I do not carry with me so much cash. Suppose I suggest £100. How do you see that? Too little?' Aubrey nodded.

'What about £150?'

'I'm no expert,' said Aubrey, 'but I imagine it's worth a little more.'

'Well,' said Johannes with a smile, 'I should like to have that watch. What would you say to £200? That is all the English money in my wallet. If that is not enough then I must give you guilders or a cheque on the Rotterdamse Bank.'

'Why do you want this particular watch?' Aubrey asked.

'I must tell you. It is possible that it is of my great-grandfather. Look here at the inscription. My name is Johannes van Dijk. My great-grandfather was Pieter van Dijk. He worked all his life in Zuid-Beveland. Middleburg is in that part of Nederland. If the watch is truly of my great-grandfather, then it should be of great sentimental value.'

* * * * *

The previous year when Johannes came to England he had lunched with Wouter de Veen, a friend from his university days, who had a senior position with Hudson Smith, Briggs & Co. Wouter had described Aubrey Pembleton-Smythe and how vain he was about his pocket watch. When he was showing it off, Wouter had noticed the inscription. When Johannes heard about the watch, he asked Wouter to let him know the date and time of Aubrey's next visit to Bristol. So on this morning, Friday the 13th March 1959, in Wouter's private office, Johannes listened to what his friend could tell him about de Mijnheer Aubrey Pembleton-Smythe.

Afterwards the two friends reminisced and swapped stories over a lunch of bread, Gouda cheese and coffee until Wouter's phone rang at 1:20 p.m. 'He's leaving now,' said Wouter. They shook hands and Wouter led the way out. At the office doorway, Wouter waved to the young Officer from the Inland Revenue Investigation Department as she hurried towards the front of the building. As he stepped into the sunshine Johannes saw the young lady climbing into a taxi at the top of the street. He would have liked to share it with her but it was already moving off and maybe it was not going to the railway station.

'Do you think that's the watch of your great-grandfather?' Wouter had asked as they shook hands again at the front door. 'Ya, I believe it,' said Johannes.

* * * * *

'Your great-grandfather's watch. I see. In that case,' said Aubrey, with a wave of his hand, 'it would be churlish of me to hold on to it. It's yours for £200. I expect it's worth more but guilders would be no use to me. And I decline most cheques even if they are in Pounds Sterling and drawn on the Bank of England in Threadneedle Street.'

Johannes smiled broadly, shook Aubrey firmly by the hand and counted all twenty £10 notes from his wallet. 'Please,' he said, handing over the cash. But before Aubrey could detach the watch from its solid silver chain Johannes said, 'It's possible the chain was also of my great-grandfather. I hope you include it in the price, yes? Thank you.' With a slight grimace, Aubrey handed over the rare antique watch and solid sterling silver chain. Johannes again shook hands and settled back into his seat to study his purchase.

Pieter van Dijk, his great-grandfather, had served the Gemeente (municipality) in South Beveland as Waterbouwkundig Ingenieur (hydraulic engineer) for 35 years from 1878 to 1913. The watch had been given 'in dankbaarheid voor uwe trouwe dienst' (in gratitude for your loyal service). Much of Nederland (meaning below land or beneath sea level) would be underwater if it were not protected by the dikes designed, built and maintained by the hydraulic engineers.

Johannes realised that his great-grandfather had been held in high esteem. The pocket watch had been extremely expensive even in 1913. Now it was worth a very great deal. The pawnbroker had not known his business. Johannes estimated its value at more than £6000. What a bargain at £200! And he really did buy it for sentimental reasons. He would give it to his son when he would be Dr. Ing. Piet van Dijk.

Unaware that he could have done much, much better than a £200 return over two years on his original £17.50 investment, Aubrey settled back into his seat. He was sure he'd sold his watch too soon but was also sure Baron Rothschild would have approved. When asked how he had become so wealthy, the Baron is said to have replied: "I always sold too soon." Was this Baron Nathan Rothschild, trading in London during the Napoleonic era? Perhaps. Aubrey turned to the page where he placed the free bookmarker from George's – the University Bookshop at the top of Park Street – and continued reading.

The start of the Rothschild banking empire may be traced back to an Ashkenazi Jew called Moses Amschel Bauer who was a shrewd money lender and owner of a counting house in Frankfurt, Germany. His son, Mayer Amschel Bauer, eventually took over his father's business. He changed his name to Mayer Amschel

Rothschild and in 1770 he married seventeen year-old Gutele Schnaper. They had five daughters and five sons: Amschel, Salomon, Nathan, Kalmann and Jacob. It is reputed that Mayer became extremely wealthy through a mixture of embezzlement, cunning and ruthless business transactions with various heads of state. All five sons became wealthy bankers and were made barons by the Austrian Emperor Francis I.

Aubrey was pleased to note that Mayer changed his name but envious of his ten children. At 51 and still unmarried, he had no hope of siring a Pembleton-Smythe banking dynasty. He'd been too young for the First World War and unfit for duty in the Second World War. Deep down Aubrey knew that even if he'd been wearing an officer's uniform young ladies still would not have given him a second glance. That's why he was puzzled by the looks the young lady opposite had given him.

* * * * *

4. down – Wet fields of grass – 5.

Rachel checked the answer to 1. across - *tax evasion*. So the second letter of 4. down is 'e'. The last letter is probably 's'. Ah, yes! It's 'meads' – derived from meadows. Now she remembered. Temple Meads station! That's where the Knights Templar built their Holy Cross Church in the 12th century. And there were water meadows in the Temple Parish. She looked up to see Aubrey staring at her over his half-moon glasses. Quickly looking away to her right she saw Johannes had closed his eyes. Turning to her left she saw Daphne had almost finished a pink bootie. On the other side of the table by the window the student was smiling to himself.

In 1932, after she received her master's degree, Mary Peters Atchison married her professor, Louis Frederick Fieser, who was twenty years her senior. She died in 1997 outliving her husband by twenty years. Together as co-authors, they published eight textbooks and the first seven volumes of Reagents for Organic Synthesis – known to chemists simply as "Fieser and Fieser." What fascinated Bob most was their descriptions of chemistry applied to medicine.

Diethyl ether – known by the public simply as "ether" or "that hospital smell" – was first used as a general anaesthetic in 1842. It boils at 34.6°C (below our body temperature of 37°C) and may be used to numb the skin prior to an injection.

Ether is highly inflammable and forms an ignitable mixture with air even at -45°C, its flash point. A refrigerator where ether was inadvertently stored exploded when the door was opened; an electrical spark from the interior light switch had ignited the ether-air mixture inside. The person opening the door was severely injured.

Dentists stopped using ether as an anaesthetic because their patients often woke suddenly and unexpectedly.

'Woke with a bang when the anaesthetic exploded!' thought Bob looking at the canvas bag on the table in front of him. Before he could start worrying about what was in his hold-all, the compartment door slid open. *'Refreshments. Anyone for refreshments?'*

'No thank you,' said Daphne politely. Rachel shook her head. Aubrey never looked up from his book. Johannes opened his eyes. 'You have black coffee?'

'Certainly. Sugar?'

'No thank you.'

'One and thruppence please.'

'One shilling and three pence, yes?' said Johannes, giving him a two-shilling coin.

'Thank you sir. That's ninepence change.'

'Daylight robbery,' said Aubrey. 'The railway's run by a bunch of crooks.'

Rachel couldn't suppress a laugh - Pembleton-Smythe of all people saying that!

Johannes smiled at her and said, 'Ya, it's terrible.'

'It does seem expensive,' said Rachel.

'No, sorry. I mean the coffee. It tastes terrible,' said Johannes with a laugh.

The train came to a halt and they heard, 'Westbury. This is Westbury. Change here for Dilton Marsh and Warminster.'

* * * * *

'Were you taking a nap just now?' asked Rachel.

'No. I just thinking with my eyes closed. This pocket watch started me to remember my family and my country.'

'Is it a family heirloom?'

'Yes, I think it is of my great-grandfather. I did not know him. He died before I was born of course. I must have known my grandfather but I don't remember him. I was very young when he died. My father is very old now but he might recognise the watch. He never spoke to me about it.'

'What will you do with it now?'

'If it *was* of my great-grandfather, then I shall keep it for when my son receives his doctorate. It should be special to him because he is an hydraulics engineer like his great-grandfather. He's a very good student. Already is he *Doctorandus*. Piet is very serious like his mother. If she were alive she would be very proud of him.'

Rachel wanted to ask him when and how his wife died but instead she said, 'Where do you live in The Netherlands?'

'So,' said Johannes, 'you do not say Holland. You know Holland is just a part of Nederland, yes? Actually it's common even for Dutch people to say Holland when they should say Nederland'

'If I remember correctly,' said Rachel, 'Holland is a province of The Netherlands.'

'Actually, North Holland and South Holland are two of the twelve provinces. Amsterdam is in the northern province. Rotterdam, where I live, is in the southern province. Have you ever been to Holland?' he asked, stressing 'Holland' with a mischievous grin.

'No, I'm sorry to say.'

'Then you must visit us and I shall be your guide in Rotterdam. That's only fair after all. You are going to be my guide in Bath Spa, yes?

Rachel blushed and said, 'What's Rotterdam like? Tell me about it.'

'Rotterdam – or dam on muddy water – was beautiful until on 10 May, 1940. That's when die Deutsche Luftwaffe started bombing to force my country to surrender. The Centrum was almost completely destroyed. Rotterdam became, as we say, the city without a heart. I shall show you Ossip Zadkine's famous statue – Stad Zonder Hart – of a person in torment with a large hole in the body. The war was terrible. The occupation was terrible. Ah, we don't talk about it.'

'Rotterdam is already being rebuilt better than before,' continued Johannes. 'We have there the largest commercial port in Europe. Now! I must not talk about business. I think you prefer history, yes? If you like museums then we have many including for architecture, art, culture, maritime, natural history and so forth. We even have a tax and custom museum.'

'You're joking, surely,' exclaimed Rachel.

'Echt waar. It's really true,' Johannes laughed. 'We have it since October 1937 but I think you would prefer our shops, yes? We'll take you to the Lijnbaan. It's a big shopping centre with streets for pedestrians only. Opened in 1953, they are the first ones in the Netherlands.'

96

'Listen,' he said, 'here is my card.'

'What does *Johannes van Dijk – Antiek, Kunst, Juwelen, Boeken en Horloges* mean?'

'It means I'm an old, crafty man who likes jewels and watches.'

Rachel laughed. 'No, really. What do those words mean?'

'Antique(s), Art, Jewellery, Books and Watches. I have a little shop in Rotterdam. Actually, I have twelve little shops – one in each province of Nederland. Please, do you have a card?'

'No, sorry,' said Rachel.

'No matter,' said Johannes, 'Please, write your name, address and telephone number on the back of one of my cards. Oh, by the way you must call me Jan.'

'The train will be stopping at Salisbury in a minute. I'll do it then.'

* * * * *

When the train stopped, Rachel wrote down her details and gave back the card.

'Thank you,' said Johannes. 'We shall correspond and make arrangements.' Then looking out of the window he said, 'Why do you say *Soulsbree* when the name is spelt S-a-l-i-s-b-u-r-y? Dutch has rules for speaking and spelling. The ij in my name always sounds the same – something like your 'ay' in 'hay'. English has no rules. In bough, cough, ought, thorough and through, the 'ough' is different every time. Sorry. I am rude. Please tell me about Salisbury.'

Salisbury Cathedral is over 700 years old. It's a masterpiece of Early English architecture. The spire is the tallest in Britain. Remembering the words on Jan's card Rachel said, 'John Constable painted the spire and surrounding countryside in some of his famous landscapes. The Cathedral has a large mechanical clock. It was installed in 1386 and is the oldest of its kind in Britain. The library has the best preserved copy of the Magna Carta, issued by King John's chancery in 1215.' Jan was staring at her.

'Am I boring you?' said Rachel nervously. Jan smiled, knowing that there was also one copy in Lincoln Cathedral and two copies were in the British Library.

'No,' Johannes replied, 'you interest me. Please, tell more,' She blushed.

'Tickets! Tickets please!' they heard the guard call out. He glanced into their compartment then continued along the corridor. 'Next stop Romsey! Romsey next stop!'

Rachel was quietly telling Jan about The Haunch of Venison – a hostelry at least 600 years old. In 1320 it housed the craftsmen working on the Cathedral spire. Aubrey was engrossed in the machinations of the Rothschilds. Daphne was trying to decide what colour to choose – blue or pink - for the third bootie. Bob was deep in Fieser and Fieser's account of the ether synthesis developed by Alexander Williamson in 1850. Then it happened.

Bob heard this sudden noise – muffled but quite loud – from his hold-all. He peeped over the top of his book. To his dismay the almost empty bag was quickly swelling up to its full size. At the same time, jets of what looked like steam or thin white smoke were pouring out of the gaps in the zip's teeth all along the top of the bag.

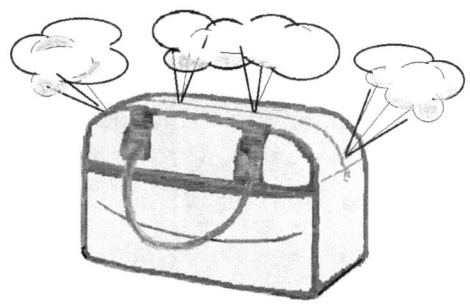

The jets were accompanied by a gentle whistling; it was like the sound of an elderly man sucking air between his teeth. After what seemed an eternity but was probably only a minute or two, the bag began slowly to collapse. Finally it lay flat and still on the table. Bob listened. All he could hear was the wheels of the train – diddle-dee, diddle-dee, diddle-dum – running on the track.

* * * * *

Daphne was frowning at her knitting pattern when she became vaguely aware of the noise. A few moments later a draught of very cold air ran over her legs and feet. She shivered and the expression "blue with the cold" came to mind. She reached for her blue wool. Then she looked up and wondered what was happening to that handsome student's bag. The train was just coming into Romsey. She would have to be quick to finish this second blue bootie before they reached Southampton.

Rachel heard the noise and turned to see what Jan was looking at. 'Incredible,' whispered Jan, as the bag inflated, gave off steam like a whistling kettle and slowly collapsed. 'It's that student's bag,' whispered Rachel. 'He's studying chemistry at Bristol University. It's probably a Rag Week stunt. In two weeks it will be Easter and students will be on holiday.'

Aubrey nodded agreement and thought to himself, 'Students ought not to waste their time and the tax-payer's money. They should be studying.' As he went back to his book he heard Rachel explain to Jan how much money Rag Week raises for charities.

* * * * *

When the train arrived at Southampton Central, Aubrey was standing in the corridor ready to get off. Without so much as a nod to his fellow passengers, he'd left the compartment, unaware that he would have to face the Inland Revenue's Miss Rachel Wallace, B.Econ., in his office on Monday morning. Bob was still buried in his textbook when Jan and Rachel said goodbye to Daphne.

'So, Rachel,' said Jan, 'you will come to Rotterdam?'

She smiled. 'I'll write and let you know.'

When they had gone Bob smiled at Daphne over the top of his textbook. 'Goodbye young man,' she said, 'Don't work too hard.' Frank was waving excitedly to her from the platform. 'I wonder.' she said to herself. 'Have a got to knit a second pink bootie?'

When she had gone, Bob opened his bag and noticed a wet, icy-cold plug of cotton wool amongst the shattered remains of his thermos flask. 'So much for wanting to show them liquid air,' he sighed when he saw his mum and dad waiting on the platform.

* * * * *

Epilogue

After a snack lunch in the undergraduate refectory on that unlucky Friday, the 13th, Bob had returned to the chemistry department where he filled his thermos flask with liquid air. He put a loose plug of cotton wool in the open neck to prevent liquid spilling out but still allow air from the evaporating liquid to escape. He placed the flask in the middle of his canvas hold-all and kept it upright with his pyjamas. So why did the flask explode?

The cotton wool became damp and the very cold air escaping from the flask turned the moisture into ice. Gradually the space between the cotton wool fibres filled with ice until the plug became one solid block of ice sealing the flask tight shut. The air could no longer escape. Pressure inside gradually rose until the flask exploded under the strain. The 'steam' coming from the bag was a fog (tiny water droplets in the air) formed when the evaporating liquid air instantly cooled the moist air in the compartment. Fortunately nobody was hurt.

According to Bob, the other passengers in the compartment either did not notice or pretended not to notice the bag's antics. We assumed this to be an example of the stiff upper lip that had helped the British survive two World Wars in the 20th century.

I suppose our 21st century Health & Safety at Work Act Regulations would today deter Bob from taking a thermos of liquid air out of the chemistry building let alone from carrying it in a bag onto a train. Nevertheless, I like to think that our 21st century British upper lip would be just as stiff now as it ever was and that the passengers in that railway compartment would remain calm and unruffled at the sight of an inflating, steaming bag.

Incidentally, when you cool rose petals and pieces of rubber in liquid air they will shatter into pieces like glass. Bob's pyjamas luckily did not suffer that fate!

Keep reading for an excerpt from the first story in Volume 2 of Michael C. Cox's collection of short stories

Facts and Fantasies

available from Amazon as an individual volume or part of the

Omnibus Collection of Short Stories

in paperback and electronic book form

* * * * *

THE BEST LAID SCHEMES

My parents, like many people after World War II, did not have a car. I was fortunate. John, a friend of mine, taught me to drive his small Morris Oxford which he used for work. He was a travelling door-to-door brush salesman. John liked some of the people he met but disliked the job, so he eventually went back to work for an insurance company. He disliked that work rather less but some of his co-workers rather more. The idea for this story stems from my recollection of John's account of life as a salesman and an insurance clerk.

* * * * *

Sitting in his little car watching the sleet sliding down the windscreen, Alan White was wondering why he ever gave up his job with the Prudential Insurance Company. Their new building, on the corner of Wine Street in Bristol, opened in 1957 just a few months before he was taken on as a junior clerk. He would travel to the office by bus – a 15-minute ride – and be one of the first to sign in. His desk was in a corner next to a radiator. On a cold afternoon he could warm his outer coat before leaving the building. If his raincoat was wet when he arrived, it would be dry and warm when he left. The pay was good. With his Christmas bonus he could treat his father, Bill, to some pipe-tobacco and his mother, Ethel, to a bottle of port. So why did he quit?

* * * * *

Clerical work was dull. Little broke the daily routine. Now and then Eddie Warburton, the office comedian, might roar with laughter and read out loud from a claims form.

> *I thought my window was down but found it was up when I put my head through it.*

From time to time an attractive secretary-typist would pop in, smile and say hello as she dropped a new file on Alan's desk. On a rare occasion the senior clerk might put his head around the door and announce the opening of a new branch. This raised everybody's hopes of a change and a promotion but such hopes were short-lived. Anyway, Alan knew that even if he rose to the dizzy heights of senior clerk or assistant branch manager, he would still feel unfulfilled.

The tedious routine was a factor but only a minor one in his decision to quit. The major factor was that he fell foul of his co-workers. Alan was very serious-minded and could be rather shy. According to at least three long-serving clerks, he was also too honest for his own good. These three so-called colleagues came to their conclusion not long after Alan's mother was taken ill.

* * * * *

Rachel Wallace first met Rupert Coleman as she was leaving the Queens Road Branch of Lloyds Bank for her lunch break. He'd held the door open and stepped out in the sunshine with her. He said hello and disappeared. Later he re-appeared in the university refectory and asked if he might share her table. It never occurred to her that he wasn't a Bristol graduate or that their second encounter wasn't a coincidence. And it didn't strike her as particularly odd that he'd forgotten his wallet and let her pay for his coffee and sandwich lunch. As they stepped into University Road, he mentioned that he had two tickets for a piano recital at the Colston Hall that evening. 'Would she like to go?' She was flattered and she was free, so she said yes.

She waited for him that evening by the fountain in front of the Victoria Rooms. She had arrived a few minutes early. On the dot of six o'clock, he appeared from behind the fountain. 'Have I kept you waiting?' Before she could reply, he said, 'You look lovely.' Then he kissed her on the cheek. 'The recital starts at 7 o'clock so we've plenty of time. Do you mind walking?' Rachel, still blushing, said truthfully, 'No. I like walking.' They went along Queens Road into Park Row as far as the Christmas Steps. From there he held her hand as they walked down to Colston Street.

Denis Matthews began his recital with Mozart's Sonata in B Flat (K333) followed by Beethoven's Sonata in C Major Opus 53 (Waldstein). Rachel admired his formidable technique and prolific memory but found both works a little heavy going. In the interval over coffee, Rupert told her that the B Flat Sonata was one of a set of four that Mozart composed after his return to Salzburg from Paris in 1779. 'He may have written them for the mademoiselles Aloysia and Constanze Weber,' said Rupert, 'before he settled on marrying Constanze.'

Rachel liked the variety in the second half. She was not familiar with the six Bulgarian Dances by Bela Bartok but she knew Schumann's Kinderschenen – subtitled, according to the programme notes, *Scenes of Childhood from Strange Lands and Peoples*. When Denis Matthews was playing no.7 – Traümerei (Dreaming) and no.11 – *Fürchtenmachen* (Frightening), Rupert's long slender fingers seemed to be playing along on his knees.

As she listened to the three intermezzos and the rhapsody in E flat Op. 119/4 by Johannes Brahms, Rachel recalled the Dutchman, Johannes van Dijk, she'd met on the train to Southampton. He had sent her a picture postcard of Ossip Zadkine's statue - Stad Zonder Hart (city without heart) - from Rotterdam and promised to write her a letter.

She saw quite a bit of Rupert after that concert. They went out several times and he always walked her home. She allowed him to kiss her goodnight but absolutely refused to allow his hands to explore her body. Rachel was determined to be virgo intacto when she walked up the aisle to marry 'Mr. Right'. After her first rebuff, Rupert kept his hands to himself and seemed content with a goodnight kiss.

She enjoyed his company. He was charming, witty and fascinating when he talked about music. What she found less adorable was his readiness to borrow money and forget to pay her back. She was beginning to wonder how honest and trustworthy he was. And then one day his name cropped up during her investigations at Lloyds Bank.

FACTS AND FANTASIES – Volume 2

1. The best laid schemes

My parents, like many people after World War II, did not have a car. I was fortunate. John, a friend of mine, taught me to drive his small Morris Oxford which he used for work. He was a travelling door-to-door brush salesman. John liked some of the people he met but disliked the job, so he eventually went back to work for an insurance company. He disliked that work rather less but some of his co-workers rather more. The idea for this story stems from my recollection of John's account of life as a salesman and an insurance clerk.

2. What are the chances?

Certain people and chance events change our lives. They make us reconsider our beliefs, discard our old habits and gain a new sense of purpose and direction. This true story is about my father and an event that achieved quite the opposite. It gives credence to the adage 'Old habits die hard' and, dare I say it, to the adage 'You can't teach an old dog new tricks.' In regard to the first, I fear that I follow in my father's footsteps.

3. A mixed blessing

This story is a confession of a crime I committed out of false pride and in a moment of weakness more than forty years ago. By now both the statute of limitations and the statute of repose have probably run out and the long arm of the law in England is unlikely to reach across the Atlantic Ocean to Canada but, to be on the safe side, I ask you to believe the name of my victim and the associated geographical details to be pure fiction.

4. The lawnmower

This is a true story. By that I mean I have described a real incident to the best of my ability and memory. However, I have not disclosed the names of the real people involved. Any former friends and neighbours who think they recognise themselves and take exception to being excluded or included will, I trust, accept my apologies and neither strike me from their Christmas card list nor add me to their to-be-sued list.

FACTS AND FANTASIES – Volume 3

1. Deception and a deadly switch

The truth underlying this story is the foolish unsecured loans that two colleagues and I made to a former colleague and his brother in 1991. The name of the school, the names of the two companies and the names of the characters, apart from my own, are fictitious. I definitely lost money. I believe I was deceived. I think it best not to comment further.

2. A gorilla in the cupboard

This story concerns a real event I witnessed and a likely consequence I imagined. I have not named the school where this occurred or used the real names of the teachers and pupil concerned in order, hopefully, to avoid costly legal actions. To any former colleagues who were also witness to the event and who might think themselves unfavourably portrayed in my story, may I assert that the names and characters are the product of my imagination and any resemblance to actual persons, living or dead, is entirely coincidental.

3. Water of life

The Bristol-Bordeaux family-to-family exchange began in 1947 with one teacher and twenty-seven pupils from Fairfield Grammar School. The scheme rapidly expanded. In the Easter of 1951, more schools – my own included – were involved and more than one hundred pupils took part - myself included – even though I was no longer studying French. In April 2007, the exchange scheme celebrated its 60th year jubilee.

4. What the eye does not see

My wife and I once owned some timeshare at Castillo Beach Club, a resort on the lower slope of a hill overlooking Caleta de Fuste on Fuerteventura in the Canary Islands. The reception, bar and restaurant were in the main area known as Lake. The other area, known as Moon, was on the other side of the Calle de Virgen de Guadalupe. There are still squirrels on Chipmunk Hill. The supermarket (El Supermercado) and restaurant (El Papagayo) may still operate. I am not sure. The characters and events in this story are pure fantasy but the settings are real enough.

FACTS AND FANTASIES – Volume 4

1. The apple cart

The small retailer has not yet been entirely driven to the wall by the supermarket chain. Some have survived as street traders in open markets which have become popular tourist attractions, e.g. Petticoat Lane in London and Albert Cuypstraat in Amsterdam. In our house here in Canada we still have knick-knacks from flea markets as far afield as the Canary Islands, France and Mexico. This story was conceived as a small tribute to stall owners we encountered around the world. As my research and writing proceeded, it became a tribute to my Canadian friends and SEARIC - their charitable Society for the Education and Assistance of Rural Indian Children.

2. Across a crowded room

On the 6th of August 2010, on the cruise liner Celebrity Constellation, Maureen and I celebrated our Golden Wedding Anniversary. This is the story of how I met my wife. Some of my scientific friends suggest we travel through life encountering people haphazardly as particles collide according to Einstein's mathematical theory of random walk. Maureen and I met by chance they say. Some of my non-scientific friends suggest otherwise. It was kismet they say. Whatever the case, of one thing I can be absolutely sure, I am glad we met.

3. The disappearing chemistry teacher

The central incident in this story occurred in 1960 during my first year of full-time teaching and is described as accurately as my memory will allow. I have given fictitious names to the school and the people involved just in case the long arm of the law could stretch 50 years back in time and instigate prosecutions under the 1974 Health and Safety at Work Act.

4. An alarming business

This story is set in Broadstone, Dorset, where I lived and worked from the Easter of 1971 until I moved to Canada in December 2000. The characters and their goings-on are figments of my imagination but inspired by certain events in which I was involved and by some people whom I held in high regard and about whom I should not, nay would not intentionally write a libellous word.